Come Together
By
Jerrie Alexander

COME TOGETHER

First edition. July 7, 2024.

Copyright © 2024 Jerrie Alexander.

ISBN: 979-8227682024

Written by Jerrie Alexander.

My Beta readers, thank you, don't sound strong enough. You rock. I'm so lucky to have your support and honesty. You are truly dear friends. You stuck with me through the years of darkness, believed in me, and I appreciate each of you.

Eve Arroyo, editor extraordinaire, I love your honesty and brilliant mind. You always ask the right questions, putting me back on point when the story stumbles.

Brynna Curry, thank you for your talent and fantastic patience and for designing my beautiful book covers.

Julie, the Formatting Fairy from Heaven, you are so very gracious and helpful. You handled all my changes with grace and patience.

Prologue

Chelsea

I'd met Taylor Horne several times while he was in college and working as a limo driver for the Club Silken, Gloss, and Gallants owners. The first time, he'd driven one of my best friends, Morgan Kimball, shopping. Not wanting to go alone, she'd invited our best friend Kayla Britton and me to go with her. Morgan had just started dating Zack Pierce, the co-owner of Silken, a members-only BDSM club. She was looking for an outfit that would knock him on his ass.

Taylor had chauffeured us to a boutique that sold adult toys and clothes. I couldn't take my eyes off him. He was tall, drop-dead handsome, and filled out his black suit perfectly. No doubt, I acted like a schoolgirl right before her first kiss.

A lot has happened since then. Morgan married Zack, Kayla is engaged to Nick Bianco, and I'm concentrating on earning a job promotion.

The admin for the company's president is retiring, and I hope to fill that position. My last raise placed me at seventy-five thousand a year, but if I'm selected for this new role, my salary will jump another ten, maybe fifteen thousand. My heart rate jumps just thinking about it.

I haven't heard a lot about Taylor until recently. He was touring Europe after taking a year off as a reward for getting his master's degree in Finance and Accounting. Now he's home, and Zack's throwing him a party.

I've taken special care with my makeup and hair tonight, chosen a dress that shows off my figure and am wearing sandals to highlight my new nail polish. My palms get damp as I thank the Uber driver. I don't know why I'm nervous. There's no reason for Taylor Horne to remember me.

Chapter 1

Chelsea

I smooth my hands down the front of my yellow sundress and walk into the entryway of Zack and Morgan's home. I've been here before, but with all the oversized windows and white marble, the foyer is still a little intimidating.

Morgan and I used to live in the same apartment building. We laughed, cried, worried, and took care of each other for years. We stay in touch by phone and are still close. She's scouted men for me for over a year, searching for the right Dom to bring me into the lifestyle she shares with Zack. I've never expressed any interest in BDSM, though, and I breathe easier knowing she's agreed to stop looking.

Judging from the low buzz of voices and the sound of music, Taylor Horne's welcome home pool party is in full swing. The main thing I remember about him is he's gorgeous. Well, he was the last time I saw him.

Unsure of how many people I'll know, I make the rounds saying hello, then locate and hug Kayla, who's walking toward the back patio.

"Grab a drink and join us at the pool," she says before disappearing into the crowd.

I found an opening and spotted Morgan and Zack. She waves and then points to an empty deck chair next to her.

I wiggle my fingers at her and start walking to the bar. I plan to lean back, relax, and watch the festivities.

Suddenly, a hand catches my arm and turns me around. My sandals slip on the marble floor, and I lose my balance but don't fall. Instead, I'm wrapped in the arms of the traveler himself.

"You weren't going to say hello?"

I look up into the piercing blue eyes I'd recognize anywhere. Eyes are impossible to forget since I've used Taylor's image while pleasuring myself many times. I untangle myself from the guest of honor's arms and step back to see if he's still as hot as I remember. My heart flutters, and my body tingles. Hoping I'm not drooling, I pull my mind out of the bedroom.

"Do you usually knock down people just to get a hello?"

"You slipped, and I saved you." Taylor smiles, showing off perfectly formed lips, the kind you can sink into and lose yourself. "Don't I get credit for that?"

"Thank you, and welcome home." I return his grin, thinking he's changed. He looks different but the same. A newfound maturity in his eyes sets my heart thumping against my chest.

"Chelsea..." he says, steering me away from the pool. "I'm sorry, but I don't know your last name."

"Coffman."

"Nice to finally meet you, Chelsea Coffman."

"Most people call me Chels."

"Chelsea is a better name for such a beautiful woman."

I roll my eyes, but love that he's so obviously flirting. "Please."

"That was bad, wasn't it?"

"The worst."

"Let me make it up to you. I'll buy you a drink. "

I can't help myself as I smile up at him. "Gracious of you since it's an open bar." God, he smells good. It's a faint scent; I want to lean into him a little. "How was your trip through Europe?"

"Amazing. Enlightening. Learning about different cultures was great. The beaches were beautiful, and the cities were full of things to see and do. Have you been?"

I shake my head. "My travel experience is limited to Hawaii, but I'd love to tour Europe someday."

"I met many interesting people, but I think it would've been more fun if I'd had someone with me." He's looking down at me with a sexy smile.

He can't know I want to run my fingers over every inch of his body or that my panties are getting damp just standing this close to him. Can he? I gather myself and pretend he doesn't set my lady parts on fire.

"I understand you're going to work for Zack Pierce. When do you start?"

"Monday. He's given me a few accounts to review in my spare time. I'll need a break from all that reading, though. May I call you, maybe take you to dinner?"

"I'd like that."

We exchange phone numbers while we wait in line at the bar. I ignore the urge to smirk at two women raking their gazes over him. Taylor's year touring

Europe has earned him a tan and sandy, sun-bleached hair, which is longer than I remember. It's tousled as if he just got out of bed. He'd make a great model with his chiseled jaw, straight nose, and height. He's wearing board shorts, sandals, and a blue T-shirt, and it's clear his body is muscular. His eyes make me feel as if he can read my thoughts.

His gaze drops to my chest, then back up. "This is a pool party. Are you wearing your bathing suit under your dress?"

"No, and I didn't bring one. I'm more of an observer." Looking around, I wish I'd at least worn shorts.

"That's a shame."

His comment dies because it's our turn to order drinks. I get a glass of red wine, and Taylor chooses a Coors.

"Where were you headed when I almost knocked you down?"

"So, you admit it."

"I got your attention, didn't I? Now, where were you going?"

"Morgan waved me toward the pool. I think she's saved a spot for me."

His hand moves to my lower back. "Maybe we'll find two chairs."

"Maybe." I don't know him, yet my body thinks we're old friends. Does it make me a slut or just horny that I'd leave with him right now if he asked?

"Something wrong?"

"Frankly, I'm surprised you remember me."

"Of course I do. If you hadn't come tonight, I would've asked Morgan for your number."

"Why?"

"Because you're gorgeous."

"Right." Now I know he's full of crap. "My mousy brown hair and boring hazel eyes drew you to me?"

"Your hair is coffee with cream, and your eyes are emerald. We won't get into what I think of your body. At least not here."

I roll my eyes at his flattery. "I think I need to sit."

"That's twice you've done that."

"Done what?"

"Rolled your eyes at me. I know you remember the day in your apartment's parking lot. I delivered you home after your shopping trip with your friends and helped you get out of the limo. You walked away but stopped and looked back. Our eyes locked. You felt it. I *know* you did."

I like that he's persistent. "I can't argue with that, but that was long ago."

"My body would recognize yours regardless of how long it's been."

I keep my mouth shut while we walk outside to where Morgan and Zack sit.

Morgan jumps out of her chair and grabs me like we didn't just talk yesterday. She's beaming at her husband as he stands and hugs me, too. If there's such a thing as the perfect couple, it's Morgan and Zack. He stands, then leans over and kisses his wife.

"Chels, why don't you keep Morgan company while Taylor and I make the rounds? I want to be sure I've introduced him to everyone."

"Hold up, Zack." Taylor looks at me and mouths the word *sorry*. "I'll be back. You'll be here, right?"

"Of course."

"And have that dinner with me I mentioned?"

"I'd like that." I'm pleased he's serious about wanting to see me again.

He winks and walks away with Zack. I set my wine on the table between Morgan and me. Then I turn to face her.

"Holy shit. I *knew* Taylor would be excited to see you." Morgan swings her feet to the tile flooring, reaches over, and smacks me on the knee. "He was eye-fucking you right up until he walked away."

A light goes off in my brain. "You told him I thought he was hot, didn't you?"

She tucks her legs into a Lotus position and shrugs. "Maybe. Or maybe Kayla mentioned it."

I mimic her position, so we're sitting face-to-face. "One of you set me up. How embarrassing. That's why he grabbed me the second I walked through the front door. He thinks he's doing you and his new employer a favor."

"He grabbed you? Do I need to kick his ass?" A breathtakingly gorgeous man perches on the foot of my chair, awaiting my answer. He tilts his head, and a lock of thick, wavy black hair falls onto his forehead. He stares at me with pale blue eyes.

I'd met Slider at Zack and Morgan's wedding rehearsal and wedding, but this is the closest I've been to him since. With his reputation, this may be *too* close.

"Nobody grabbed me, but thanks for offering to come to my rescue." I extend my hand, which he wraps his strong fingers around.

He doesn't return my hand, though. Instead, he moves closer while his thumb strokes the underside of my wrist. "I didn't get to tell you at the wedding, but you are stunning."

"Thank you." I stare at him, dumbfounded. We hadn't interacted at Zack and Morgan's wedding; he didn't stick around for long. But I've heard all about him, except no one told me he could make angels cry with his smile.

"Slider," Morgan says. "Turn my friend's hand loose."

He releases me, stands, and walks over to her. Then he kisses the top of her head. "Great party."

"Thank you." She pets the side of his face like he's a puppy. "I'm glad you came."

"I always do." His gaze returns to me, and I sit there speechless at his double entendre.

"Don't hit on Chels," Morgan says. "Not tonight."

"Not tonight," he repeats with an audible sigh. "If you ladies will excuse me, I'm heading to the bar."

"It's nice to see you again."

"You too. Let me know when you're free. I want to show you around Gallants."

I force my jaw to stay in place as he walks away. The second he's out of hearing range, I turn to Morgan. "How did I not notice before that he looks a lot like Superman?"

She shakes her head and waves off my comment. "He doesn't have a cleft chin."

"What? Well, that's all he's missing."

"You need to stay away from him. Zack says Slider goes through women faster than a kid eating M&M's. He's already broken more hearts than most men do in a lifetime."

"Don't change the subject. I'm not saying I want to have sex with Slider, but you have to admit he's gorgeous."

"Okay. He's hot, and Zack says there's no better friend. It's well known his appetite for women is ravenous. I've seen him in action at Silken. Sex is a game to him."

I turn and lean back in the lounge chair, prop my feet up, and sip my wine. "Yeah, I get it." My thoughts drift back and forth between Slider and Taylor.

After spending an hour or so catching up with Morgan and chatting with her friends as they wander by Kayla and Nick join us. She's changed from her swimsuit into a white sundress,

highlighting her suntan. She's the social butterfly of our group and has been circulating since I got here, while Morgan and I have stayed in the same spot all night. Then Nick drags a chair close, sits, and pulls her onto his lap. She leans against him and says, "Parties are always fun but also tiring."

I nod in agreement because she's opened the door for me to excuse myself. "I enjoyed tonight, too, but I should get going."

"Sounds like I'm too late with this." Taylor steps into my line of vision, holding a glass of red wine. Zack is with him, and he hands Morgan a drink.

"It's never too late to have a beverage with friends," Kayla says. "And we haven't had a chance to talk."

"The three of us talked yesterday."

Morgan chuckles. "Okay, you got me. Yes, we did."

I take the glass from Taylor. "Thank you."

"Sorry, we got caught up talking business. I wanted to spend some time with you tonight." The sincerity in his tone impresses me.

"I'll be around, and you have my number."

"Count on a call from me." He winks, and it goes straight into my bloodstream. I don't understand why desire rolls through my body, but I can't deny it. I spend a few minutes talking with the group while I finish my wine. Then I lift my shoulders, rolling them a couple of times before setting my glass on the table and pulling my phone from the hidden pocket of my sundress.

Taylor touches my arm. "Tell me you took an Uber so I can drive you home."

I want to take him up on his offer, but I have no idea how much he's had to drink, so I make a suggestion. "Yes, I did. Maybe we can share one."

"Yes, you can ride share." Kayla's eyes light up with that devious gleam she gets when she's up to something.

In this instance, it looks like I'm that "something."

"Taylor, I think it's a good idea to leave your car here overnight," Zack says, confirming Kayla's idea.

"Sharing works for me." Taylor pulls his cell from his back pocket. His fingers hesitate. "You agree?"

"Sure."

He opens an app and returns his cell to his pocket seconds later. "Our ride will pick us up out front in nine minutes."

We say goodnight, and I hug my two best friends, who are grinning like I've been selected as bachelorette of the month. Just as we make it outside to the top of the stairs, a car pulls through the open gates. Taylor takes my hand and walks next to me as we descend. He checks with the driver, opens my door, and helps me inside. Then he makes his way to the other side, climbs in, and buckles up. I wave as our ride whisks us off the property and heads for the highway.

Taylor winks at me just as he did earlier in the evening. It occurred to me that his balance walking down the steps to the car was steady, and his eyes were clear. I crook my finger back and forth at him. He leans toward me, and I let him have it when he's a breath away. "You could have driven. You're not drunk. You're sneaky."

Instead of flinching or showing surprise, he closes the minuscule distance separating us and kisses me. God, his lips are as soft as I imagined. His touch is gentle and light. Just as I will join in on the fun, he pulls away.

"Are you pissed?"

"I can't imagine anyone being pissed at you for long." My tongue slides across my bottom lip, searching for a taste of his mouth.

"I'm glad. The last thing I want is for you to be upset with me." He holds his hand out to stop me from speaking. "Before you ask, I'm not sure why. You pull me to you like a magnet. When you're near me, my mind and body go on high alert, and I want to do all kinds of dirty things to you. I'm hoping I affect you the same way."

I'm generally not speechless. Any friend or coworker will confirm that, but I can't put together a string of words that will sound coherent. Taylor takes advantage of my silence and kisses me again. His mouth covers mine. Somebody moans and I think the sound is coming from me. His tongue dives inside, tasting me. It's sinfully erotic. I stretch against the seatbelt to meet him, wanting to hold his face in my hands. A growl rolls up from his chest. He's feeling the frustration, too. I pull away.

The driver clears his throat. "I'd tell you two to get a room, but you're almost home."

"What?" I look out the window for landmarks or signs. Judging from the building and college campus ahead of us, we're getting closer to Taylor's apartment. If I'm going to back out, now's the time.

He reaches across the back seat and covers my hand with his. "He can take you home from here, or you can go up with me. I promise nothing will happen if you don't want to."

The OMG section of my brain starts running like a calculator, adding up the months it's been since I've had sex. Oh, shit. I shaved everything that needed shaving today in the shower. Didn't I?

The car slows down and leaves the highway. I look at Taylor's face and see hope in his eyes. I nod. That's all. No comment. Nothing. I'm not a silly teenager, and it's time to prove I can decide and articulate what I want. "I don't work on Saturday. Staying the night shouldn't be a problem." I swallow back my embarrassment for assuming. "If I stay," I add quickly.

"Of course you will. You're off Saturday and Sunday, right?"

"I am, but I have scullery maid duties before Monday."

"Scullery maid duties?"

"Yeah. I clean the house, do my laundry, dust furniture, and vacuum. Stuff like that."

The driver stops in front of a small apartment complex. Taylor thanked him and helped me out of the car. Standing on the curb next to Taylor, watching our ride share's taillights fade, I'm questioning my decision's wisdom.

"You're having second thoughts about staying with me." His arm wraps around my shoulders. He's warm and strong as he massages the back of my neck. "I will never force you into anything. Say the word, and I'll call for another Uber and wait right here with you until the car picks you up and drives away."

Taylor's words sound sincere, yet mixed with disappointment. I realize I don't want to leave. Every fiber in my being wants him, so why walk away? "Which apartment is yours?"

A smile lights up his face, and he squeezes my shoulder. "I'll show you."

We walk inside to the elevator. The doors are open, and a chair is blocking the entrance. It has an out-of-order sign taped to it. His place is three floors up, so we take the stairs. Taylor unlocks his door and leads me inside. It's neat and clean, but for such a tall, broad-shouldered man, I'm surprised he doesn't feel boxed in. Maybe it's all he can afford. I remember when I had to budget my money more closely than now.

"It's too small to entertain anyone. Until now, all I've used this place for was to study and sleep."

"Don't tell me I'm the first woman who's been in your apartment."

He pulls me toward him until my chest meets his. "You're the first woman I've invited to stay the night."

Chapter 2

Taylor

Chelsea's breasts press against my chest, and her gaze locks with mine. Lowering my head, I capture her lips and crush them with a kiss while soaking up the low moan she makes. Her soft hands come up to my face and caress my cheeks. I've never experienced a rush of lust like the one that hits me. My cock hardens with the need to be inside her now. My hands grasp her ass, and I pick her up.

She wraps her legs around me. I back her toward my breakfast bar, lift her, and sit her on the edge.

She gasps, and that stops everything.

"What happened?"

"Nothing critical." She reaches up and rubs my frown away. "My bare thighs hit the cold tile."

"I thought maybe I'd left a fork or something sharp on it."

We both laugh at that.

"*That* would have cooled things down."

I scoop her up in my arms and carry her to my bedroom, sitting her on the edge of the mattress.

She stands and walks toward me. I can't quite read her facial expressions. But when she catches the hem of my T-shirt with her hands and pulls it over my head, I see the passion in her eyes.

I turn her around and ease the straps of her yellow dress off her shoulders, then kiss across her back and up her neck. She shivers and tilts her head to the side. I breathe in her scent and bury my nose in her hair. "I like strawberries."

"Taylor," she whispers, as my tongue tastes her delicate skin up her neck to her ear.

I pull the lobe into my mouth and drag my teeth over it. The zipper of her dress slides easily, allowing me to tug it downward until it lies in a puddle at her feet. I didn't think my cock could get any harder, but it does when I see she's not wearing a bra. I slide my hands around her and cup her full breasts, massaging the soft skin with my fingers. They fit perfectly in my palms. Her moan is so faint I almost don't hear it.

As soon as her feet are clear, I pick up the dress and drape it across the chair in the corner. "Turn around."

Without hesitating, she moves to face me. "You're smiling."

"Damn right, I am. I'm looking at perfection." Her panties are barely there and are flesh-colored. They almost match the color of her dusty-rose nipples. They're taut as if demanding my attention. I roll them between my thumb and forefinger.

"I think you need to be naked, too," she says in a whisper.

I release her and reach for the snap on my shorts, but she stops me.

"I'll do it."

I drop my hands to my side, ready to turn myself over to her, at least for now. She unzips my shorts and pushes them to the floor. I quickly kick them to the side. She drops to her knees and rubs her hand back and forth across my cock through my underwear.

"Fuck," I groan.

Her gaze lifts and meets mine just as she peels me bare. Her hand, soft as a rose petal, cups my cock, lowering it until it's in line with her mouth. Her pretty pink tongue darts out to slide across the swollen head, lapping up my precum. She licks me from the base to the tip before sucking me deep inside her mouth. She pulls back, then goes deep again. My hands dive into her hair, my fingertips digging into her scalp. "Take all of me, Chelsea. All of it."

She bobs up and down, her hot, wet mouth making me slicker and easier to take. She slides lower until I hit the back of her throat. Her lips are at the base of my dick, her gaze is locked with mine as she swallows, and I sink even deeper. The sensation almost buckles my knees. I don't want to pull out, but I'm holding on by a thread, so I tighten my hold on her head and lift her off me.

Then I take her face in my hands and kiss her. "That was amazing. How the fuck do you do that?"

"I don't have a gag reflex. It's weird, huh?"

"Fuck no, it's not weird. You almost brought me to my knees." I guide her to the middle of the bed. "You're an amazing woman, and I'm going to learn everything you like and don't."

"And how do you plan on doing that?" Her eyes are full of desire with a hint of mischief.

"We're going to try everything I knew before my trip to Europe and everything I learned there." I reach inside the nightstand drawer, grab a handful of condoms, and drop them on the bed.

"Your trip was educational?"

"Oh, yeah." I crawl up the bed, cradle her breasts in my hands, and rub my cheek stubble against her soft skin. I pull one nipple into my mouth and circle the tight bud with my tongue. Her hips shift when I nip the rigid peak and then lick the tip until she's moaning. I move to the left, cupping the other in my hand. "You're so beautiful. I could worship these babies all day."

"Thank you." Her cheeks flush. It's the first time I've noticed anything that embarrasses her.

I devote my attention to her breast, lashing, sucking, and massaging until she's squirming underneath me. The low sounds she makes have me so hard it's almost painful. I kiss my way to her belly button, mimicking what I'm going to do to her pussy very soon.

I slide my hands under her knees, then bend and spread them. My thumbs open her outer lips. She's bare, pink, and so wet she's glistening. Her scent rises to my nose, and I breathe in her luscious aroma. I've never wanted to taste anything as badly as I do her.

"Please. Taylor, please."

"Please, what? Tell me what you need. My tongue? My fingers? My cock?"

She lifts onto her elbows, and the passion in her eyes sends fire licking through my veins.

"Your cock. I need you inside me."

My plans to lick her until I taste her cum will have to wait. I grab a condom, tear open the package, and cover myself. I lift her feet, position them against my shoulder, and rub my throbbing cock through her juices.

"You're huge, so go slowly..." she says as the corners of her mouth lift, "at first."

I want to slam into her and fuck her until her eyes roll back in her head, but I ease the tip inside her heat. Silky skin encases my cock as I press a little further. Going slow could cause an early crisis for me, so I focus my gaze on the headboard and don't look at her. Her hips lift, taking me deeper. A growl erupts from my chest.

"Taylor, you feel so good inside me."

I dig my toes into the mattress and slam home, stopping when I bottom out against her cervix. My balls tighten, ready to empty themselves. Then I freeze. There will be more tonight, and I won't ruin things by coming sixty seconds after I start.

"Be still for a minute.

"Okay." Her eyes close, and for a minute, the only thing I hear is her breathing.

I force my brain to count backward and take a second to pull myself together. Then I flex, pulling back slowly and sliding in deep. I glance at her, and her gaze meets mine. It feels as if she sees inside me and knows my deepest needs. Then she smiles up at me. She's so fucking beautiful, my chest squeezes. Her hips lift again and press against me.

"Fuck me hard and fast. Please."

"My pleasure." I slide back until just the tip of my cock is inside her. "I'm going to fuck you over and over until neither of us can walk." My cock twitches, encouraging me to shut up and get busy satisfying her. I drop down over her, balancing on my forearms, and cover her lips with mine. Our tongues meet and tangle for domination. She makes this delicate mewl when I pull away, rise, and slide my hands under her ass. I lift her for a better angle, and I'm not gentle as I thrust again and again, going harder and faster with each stroke.

"God!" she cries out. "*So* good."

I've hit the sweet spot that will bring on an intense orgasm. I work it until she's thrashing under me, her hips matching my every move. Shifting my weight onto one arm, my hand slides between us, and my fingers find her clit. Her nails bury in my back, and her mouth opens, but no sound comes out.

"Come. I want to feel you come on my cock."

Chelsea's eyes fly open. Her gaze is wild, and her pupils are dilated. "Oh, God! Yes. Yes," she groans.

I hold off until the tingle in my lower spine warns me there's no holding back. When her pussy convulses and clamps down on me, I release. I roar as cum jets out in streams, filling the condom. I keep pounding until her body ceases to quake.

I roll over, taking her with me so she's on top and not trying to breathe under my weight. Her head falls on my sweaty chest, and I stroke her damp hair off her face. "You are spectacular. That was mind-blowing."

I can feel her smiling against my chest. "It certainly was."

I slide out from under her. "Don't move."

"I couldn't if I tried."

As I walk to the bathroom, my chest swells, knowing I've brought her an orgasm to remember. I dispose of the condom, run warm water over a washcloth, and return.

I stop a few feet from the bed.

She's smiling, dreamy-eyed, and lying where I left her. Watching her for a moment, I realize she's even more stunning than I thought. I climb in beside her and gently wash her.

"This is the first I've had this kind of attention," she says with a yawn.

"But not the last." I don't state it as a question. It's a fact.

"Good."

I toss the rag toward the bathroom, pull her back against my chest, and slide my arm around her so I can cup her soft pussy in my hand. She wiggles closer to me, pressing her ass against my growing cock. Then she turns onto her back.

"Now look what you've done." I take her hand and show her. Her fingers wrap around me and squeeze.

"And it worked?"

"I'll show you how well." I roll on top of her and slide back, forcing her legs apart. "I'm going to have the taste of your sweet pussy on my tongue when I go to sleep."

She chuckles. "We're going to sleep?"

****

I carry my coffee to the living room and turn on the TV. I'd closed the bedroom door behind me when I got out of bed, hoping to let Chelsea sleep late. With the sound turned low, I flip channels until I find a station that does not have all Saturday morning cartoons. Then, I lean back to catch up on the news. A few minutes later, I realize I don't have a clue as to what the newscaster has been saying. My mind and cock are still in bed with the sensual woman warming my sheets.

"Good morning." Chelsea comes and sits on the arm of my couch. She's barefoot, wearing the T-shirt I wore last night, and her hair is pulled up in a messy knot. She looks adorable.

"Yes, it is." I turn off the TV. "I tried not to wake you."

"I'm an early riser, too. I have to be ready for work and downtown Monday through Friday by eight."

"Me too. I'll have to get accustomed to my new schedule. Most of my classes were late morning, and a few were online." I stand and walk to the kitchen, taking my cup with me. "Coffee?"

"Yes, black, please."

I fill two mugs and carry them to the couch, placing them on the end table. I pull her off the padded arm and onto my lap. I kiss her, and she tastes like mouth wash. "You sleep okay?"

"Yeah. The only time I woke up was for the second, third, and fourth times we had sex." She leans over and kisses my forehead. "I'm not complaining."

I lean behind her and bring both cups around her, holding them out for her to choose one. "Careful. It's hot."

She lifts her drink to her mouth. "That's okay. I'll blow on it."

A puff of air skims across the liquid. It does nothing to cool me down. I know she can feel me getting hard. "Want some bacon and eggs for breakfast?"

"Sure. Wait, you cook?"

"Just the basic stuff, nothing fancy. I had to learn my way around a stove or starve. I had a few scholarships and student loans to help me, but I paid most of the college tuition myself. Going to a hamburger joint was a luxury." I slide her off my lap and walk across to my one-person kitchen. She stands and follows me. "Sit at the breakfast bar. There's not enough room for two people in here."

Chelsea perches on my barstool and watches me. "No family to help?"

"None that I would ask for money." I pull bacon, eggs, and butter from the fridge and line them up on the counter. I get the bacon started and turn back to her. "My mother has been ill for years. It's taken a toll on my father and their finances."

"That's why you chose investments?"

"Probably. But I've always been good with numbers and research. My education will allow me to be successful and make good money."

"Where do your parents live?"

"Shelbyville. It's a little over three hours from here." I take the toaster and move it in front of her with a loaf of bread, butter, and strawberry jam. "Q and A time is over. Plug that in and take charge."

She salutes me. "Yes, sir."

"I like the sound of that."

I drain the bacon from the frying pan and put it on paper towels. Then, I crack the eggs into a bowl and add salt, pepper, and a dash of milk before beating the hell out of them. I hear the toaster pop as I pour them into the frying pan.

Soft hands pat my hips. "Don't move. Just nod at the cabinet door where I can get plates."

I nod and don't move another muscle. Chelsea grabs everything we need while I dump the eggs in a bowl. I turn and block her from getting past me. "It seems you're trapped."

She lifts up on her toes and kisses my cheek. "Will that set me free?"

"It's just a down payment."

I let her squeeze by and notice she's moving like she's in pain. I guess I haven't paid attention to her walk this morning. I slide my arm around her and take her weight on me. "How did I not notice you're hurting?"

She groans. I take the stuff from her and put it on the table. I ease her down onto a chair and sit next to her. "Are you sore from too much sex? Want me to draw you a hot bath?"

"No, and not yet," she says, lifting her gaze to meet mine. She's doing her best not to laugh, but there's no hiding the sparkle in her eyes.

"I have a cure for what ails you."

She's grinning from ear to ear. Her head goes back, and her peals of laughter fill the room. "What, more sex?"

"I was thinking a spanking and then sex."

Chelsea stops laughing. "You wouldn't."

Fuck, I've gone too far too soon.

"Maybe I'll let it slide this time."

She takes a couple of slices of bacon and passes me the platter. We fix our plates and eat in silence for a minute. "Have you been to Silken?"

"Only as a limo driver. I've never gone inside." She has my attention if she wants to talk about what goes on at the club. "Have you?"

"No. Being friends with Morgan and Kayla, though, I've heard a lot about it."

"How much do you know about the lifestyle and BDSM?"

"More than you'd expect. A few years ago, it cost my friend her marriage."

I take her hand in mine. "What happened?"

"We'd been friends through college and had kept in touch after graduation. We worked close enough that we met for lunch, went shopping, and that kind of thing, but she never mentioned her lifestyle until one night when she came to my apartment in tears.

"She and her husband were into BDSM, and she loved being his submissive. After they'd been married a few years, though, he changed. He insisted that the minute she entered their apartment, she was his slave. Then he started testing her obedience."

"How?"

"He came home from work one day and informed her he'd gifted her to a coworker for the night. He would be in the room to observe the sex. She begged him not to make her, but she gave in and did as he ordered. A few weeks later, they attended a couple's party, and he told her to crawl across the room to one of the men and give him oral sex while everyone watched. She ran out of the house, called a cab, and came straight to my apartment. I wanted to pull the bastard's hair out, but she needed a friend, so I just listened."

"He was wrong on so many levels. Sub or slave, a Dom should never force anyone to do anything they don't want."

Chelsea pushes her plate away. Her gaze pins me to my chair. I've either said too much or not enough.

"I'm sorry for interrupting. Go on."

"We stayed up all night talking. I finally got her to bed in my spare room, but she spent the rest of the night crying. She was gone when I woke up the next day. I reached out to her, calling and texting. I just wanted to know if she was okay, but I never heard from her again. Maybe she was embarrassed that I knew what had happened between her and her husband."

"You were a good friend. I hate that it happened to her, and you were left with such a bad impression of the lifestyle."

"It was a long time ago. Things got busy shortly after, and I gave up trying to contact her. I was promoted to admin for the VP of Accounting. Morgan and

I were friends, and then Kayla came to work there, and life moved on. I know just by listening to them talk how happy they are and that my friend's husband was a horrible Dom, but I'm still a little skittish."

"Thank you for telling me. I'm sorry that happened to your friend. I hope it didn't leave a terrible taste in your mouth toward all Doms."

"I thought it had, but I'm rethinking my decision." She snatches the last slice of bacon, rips it in half, and feeds me a piece. "I'll wash, you dry."

She stands and readjusts her messy-bun hairstyle that looks ready to topple. My dick jumps to attention. "You could've warned me you don't have any panties on." I pull up the T-shirt and cup her naked cheeks. "You have a beautiful ass." I squeeze it a couple of times. "You're perfect."

"I'm glad you like it."

"Are you kidding?" I stand, pull her into my arms, and push my erection against her, showing her just how hard I am. "I like *everything* about you. I've wanted you since the first time I saw you, but I didn't think I could handle it all between college and work. But I wasn't interested in a one-and-done relationship with you."

She's staring at me like I've grown a second head.

Then Chelsea tugs the T-shirt down, covering her bare bottom. "I forgot, I have a meeting this morning. I should get dressed and go home."

Chapter 3

Lounging on my couch trying to watch an old movie, I feel a little guilty for eating and running this morning, but even more so for lying to Taylor. He was obviously surprised, yet he didn't question me. He just ordered me an Uber and put the cost of my ride home on his credit card.

I need to clear my head and think about last night. There's no question that he's amazing in bed. His dick is long and thick, and his stamina is off the charts. He put my wants and orgasms first, which happened multiple times. I can hear Morgan's and Kayla's reactions if I give them details about last night. Both will call me crazy for not still being in bed with him. That's precisely why I haven't answered their texts.

He's interested in more than a weekend romance, which greatly pleases me. The mention of a spanking and his comment that all Doms aren't assholes makes me believe he's interested in exploring the BDSM lifestyle. Hell, maybe he already *has* experience being a Dom. Taylor said he'd teach me everything he learned in Europe, and I don't believe he was talking about the architecture of the Parthenon or one of the many monasteries in Greece.

When the timer goes off on my washer, I walk down the hall to move the clothes to the dryer. It's a small, stacked unit just the right size for me. I mentally mark off one weekend chore that I call my scullery maid duties. I undoubtedly picked up the term from the erotic historical romances I love to read. With plans to start reading a new book I've just downloaded, I set the timer on the dryer and return to the couch.

Just as I turn on my Kindle, a rapid knock on my door interrupts my quiet. I'd showered when I first got home this morning and am currently wearing baggy cotton warm-ups and a faded Cubs T-shirt. Barefoot and braless, I pad over and look out the peephole on my door. So much for time to think or even read.

It's not even noon, and my best friends are outside, ready for all the details. I unlock the door but leave the security chain engaged. "Sorry. You aren't on today's schedule."

Morgan laughs, and Kayla attempts a scowl.

"Don't tease us. You should be proud we love you enough to drive across town to check on you."

I release the chain, open the door, and step out of the way, knowing they will enter like two fast-moving hurricanes. "Good morning."

Morgan air kisses me. "We brought food and drink."

She's carrying a sack with the name of our favorite bakery on the side. Kayla has one of the cardboard carriers from our favorite coffee shop. The aroma filling my living room takes me back to when we lived in the same apartment building.

Kayla hands me a cup of black coffee while Morgan grabs three plates and arranges them on my coffee table.

"I saw the coffee and pastry sack through the peephole. It's the only reason I opened the door."

"Lying bitch," Kayla says and laughs as she places the other two coffees next to the plates. Wearing jean shorts and a white, lacey blouse, she sits on the floor and scoots closer.

Morgan joins me on the couch. She kicks off her sandals and folds her legs under her. "Spill, woman. Tell us everything."

"Wait!" Kayla says a little too loudly, and Morgan and I freeze.

"What?" I open the bag and take a lemon cream-filled doughnut for myself. They knew caffeine and sugar would loosen my tongue.

Kayla draws an air triangle. "This is the exact seated position we were in when you and I went to Morgan's and demanded the juicy details on Zack."

I miss these two women so much that a sharp pain zips through my heart. I don't resent the love they both have found, but we were closer than some sisters back then. Our in-depth conversations on how the world was treating us, as well as our shopping trips, daily lunches, and vowing to kill the most recent guy who'd broken one of our hearts, had been a big part of my life. We'll be friends forever, but it's different now.

"Hello," Morgan says, leaning across the table and waving her hand in front of my face. "Where did you go?"

"Sorry. We did grill Morgan, didn't we?"

"Damn right," Kayla states. "Because we look out for each other."

Morgan swallows a sip of coffee. "Yes, we do, and you two were all over me. Kayla was threatening a violent procedure on Zack's genitals if he hurt me, and, Mother Chels, you were quizzing me."

"I wanted to make sure you knew what you were doing."

"And I did." Morgan's expression always changes when she talks about her husband. "I just want you to be happy."

Kayla is slowly nodding. "What she said."

I take a deep breath and blow it out. "Last night was amazing. Taylor knows his way around and inside a woman's body."

Kayla reaches over and snags a chocolate doughnut. "So, are you going to see him again?"

"I don't know." I pause and remember my short conversation with Taylor before I left his apartment. "When I abruptly announced I had to go home, he asked me what was wrong. He thought he did or said something to upset me."

Morgan moves down the couch closer to me. "What did you say to that?"

"I lied. I said I'd forgotten an appointment scheduled for today." Saying that out loud sets the coffee in my stomach churning.

"Why? You've never been shy about speaking up."

"He's looking for a serious relationship, and that scares the shit out of me. All three of us have been down that road. The guy is Mr. Romantic at first, and then one day, the bastard spots a tall, sexy blonde, and it's over. Then *we're* the ones holding each other, cussing and crying."

Morgan nods. "So you don't trust him enough to give him a shot?"

"I didn't say that."

"Maybe not to Taylor, but it's true. I can see it in your face. It's perfectly acceptable to be scared, but Zack swears that Taylor's a great guy."

"He spooked me, okay?" I close my eyes and gather myself. "I'm sorry. I have no reason to snap at you two. He said he's wanted me since the first day we met. Who feels like that and waits this long to do something about it?"

Kayla's eyebrows pull into a frown. "Did he try to push or force you into doing anything you feel is wrong?"

"Nothing like that," I tell them about my friend and her bastard husband. I'd never shared it with anyone until Taylor, and I have to wonder why I picked him to tell. "How could anyone who loved you force you to have sex with strangers?"

"The operative word was *love*. Your friend's husband needs his balls cut off." Kayla's shaking her head. "Do you really think Nick would even consider forcing me to do that?"

"Zack damn sure wouldn't. Even now, he checks to make sure I consent to things we've done a million times." Morgan's tone leaves no doubt of her belief.

"Taylor said the same thing you two are."

Morgan catches my chin and turns my head toward her. "That's a clue as to how he'll treat a woman. *Any* woman."

"He told me not to judge all Doms on the behavior of my old friend's husband." I stand and pace from my window to the balcony to the wall just past my dining room table. My mind is racing.

What if I let him tie me up, and I freak out?

It's too much to think about. The timer on my dryer going off ends my train of thought.

"We'll get out of your hair," Kayla says, finishing her coffee. Then, she and Morgan stand at the same time.

"You have a lot to think about," Morgan says as she pulls me in for a hug. "Remember, we're here for you."

Kayla then wraps her arms around me and squeezes. "I disagree. You don't have a lot to think about at all. You have one decision to make. Do you want him in your life or not?"

They go as quickly as they came, leaving me to wish I hadn't rushed away from Taylor's apartment this morning. When my cell buzzes, and I run to get it, I'm hoping it's him.

But it's from Kayla:

Chinese. Wednesday night at your place. Love you.

I text her a thumbs-up, empty the dryer, and carry my things to the bedroom, where I dump them on the bed. Thirty minutes later, I'm sitting in the same place, and not one article of my clothing has been hung, folded, or put away. I get up and start finishing my weekend chores. Cleaning doesn't require a lot of concentration, so my mind keeps returning to Taylor.

I have dry cleaning to pick up, but before I go, I shower, wash and dry my hair, and then sort through my closet. I slip on underwear, a pair of skinny jeans, and a soft knit pullover and decide on my favorite pair of tennis shoes. My phone has remained silent, but I check for calls or texts anyway. A little disappointed Taylor hasn't reached out to me, I grab my car keys, sling my purse strap over my shoulder, and walk out into a hard body that doesn't budge.

I bounce off Taylor's chest, and the only reason I don't fall on my ass is that his strong arms pull me against him.

"If this is your way of welcoming me, I like it." His deep, throaty voice weakens my knees.

"I'm going to pick up my dry cleaning."

This close to him, I have to lean my head back to see his face. His father must've been Zeus, Apollo, or Perseus—one of those mythical creatures that stood around looking big, bad, and beautiful.

"I'm happy to drive you." He's smiling at me, and all other thoughts leave my brain.

"You went after your car."

"I did. Since I was in the neighborhood, I decided to stop by and see how your meeting went."

I push off him and step back. I don't try to stop the smile spreading across my face. "How about you forgive me for lying about the meeting, and I'll forgive you for lying about being in my neighborhood?"

He releases me and steps back. "Done."

"I'm in no hurry. Come in for a minute."

He enters my apartment and looks around. "This is really nice. It's got your stamp on it."

"My stamp?"

"Sure. It's warm and cozy, unlike mine. The best way to describe my place is serviceable. If I decide to move into something larger, I want at least two bedrooms and more square footage."

"That's not asking for too much. You'll probably be able to afford it after you go to work."

"Yeah. I'm excited as hell to start earning a real paycheck."

My mind scrambles for a way to ease the tension I caused by leaving his apartment so abruptly. "Want a bowl of ice cream?"

It's lame, but it gets a smile from Taylor.

"Sure. That's my mom's favorite go-to mood stabilizer."

I breathe a sigh of relief at his relaxed tone. "It's a woman thing."

He follows me to the kitchen and watches while I get two bowls from the cabinet. I open the fridge and grab the ice cream and a bottle of chocolate syrup. "All I have is vanilla."

"Works for me." He picks up the bowls and holds them while I fill them. Then, I pop the top on the syrup and hold it over his portion. "Yes? No?"

He grins like a kid in a candy store. "Lots."

When we finished creating our homemade sundaes, I put a spoon in each and led him into the living room. Taylor sits on the couch, and once I join him, he hands me my bowl. My stomach growls loudly, protesting that I've eaten nothing but sweets today.

"What about your dry cleaning?"

I shrug it off. "They don't close until six on Saturdays."

He spoons in a mouthful and groans. "I can't remember the last time I ate ice cream."

"It's a staple for a single woman. It soothes disappointments and broken hearts."

"That's good to know."

"I'd really like you to tell me about your time in Europe."

He stops his spoon in midair. "All of it?"

My heart is about to jump out of my throat, where it's presently stuck. "You alluded to things you'd learned. Tell me about those."

*****

Taylor

"My perspective changed on a lot of things. I learned about what Zack refers to as an 'alternate lifestyle.' I've known what goes on inside Club Silken for years, and I have an open invitation from Zack to be his guest, but between school and work, I never have time for anything more than occasional sex."

I tried to read her, looking for a sign of interest or fear, but she revealed nothing. The last thing I want to do is to fuck this up and lose her completely, but I can't lie to her.

"Go on."

"My interest in BDSM became more serious after I read a magazine in Athens named *Skin Two*. I discovered sexual freedom is more readily accepted in Greece. It's more open and not hidden away in some areas, miles outside the city. When I reached the Greek island of Corfu, I made friends with a couple who introduced me to the darker, sensual side of Greece. We hit the BDSM clubs and explored fetishes, bondage, and sexual role-play. There was always somebody who willingly taught this newcomer that it's not all about whips and humiliation."

Chelsea is silent for a few moments. "What was your favorite?"

"Have you ever heard of Shibari?"

She shakes her head no but doesn't speak.

"Shibari is the ancient Japanese art of rope bondage or tying. I watched a master tie a woman in satin ribbons using different patterns. By the time he finished, her body was relaxed, and her mind seemed at peace. It was erotic and mesmerizing."

"They had sex with her tied in knots?"

I can't hold back my smile. "They did, and she was pleading for it." I haven't convinced Chelsea, so I will continue. "If you'll get your laptop, we'll look it up."

"That's a good idea." She stands and walks upstairs.

I want to follow her, but I know it would be a big mistake. I wait until she returns with her laptop and hands it to me.

"I turned it on. Let's move to the couch so we can both see the screen easily."

I do as requested. When she sits next to me, with our thighs touching, I beg my cock not to overreact at being so close to her. "Ready?"

I pull up a site with dozens of examples and instructions. Then, we read about the different types of ropes. "The master used a red silk binding sash because she was inexperienced. Shibari isn't about hurting someone or making them uncomfortable. The aim is for the woman to feel loved, cared for, and safe. She's surrendering herself to the other person and permitting herself to let go."

I glance at Chelsea and discover she seems enthralled with the pictures and explanations.

"Did you see this? The ropes and knots are positioned to stimulate the body's pressure points and erogenous zones." She turns her head to look at me, and I see the heat in her eyes.

Fuck, this is great.

"Before you get too interested, I didn't learn to do any patterns. There are classes you can take to become a master, but my time was up, and I had to come home."

"Too bad. But it helps me understand a lot more than I did."

I'm hard as steel by this point, and her showing interest in BDSM makes it worse. "Good." I clear my throat. "We should go pick up your dry cleaning."

She closes her laptop, puts it on the coffee table, and turns to face me. Then, she blinks rapidly and tilts her head. Her smile is full of mischief. "Hey, Taylor."

"Hey, Chelsea."

She points at my swollen cock. "We need to take care of that first."

"Believe it or not, I didn't come over here for sex."

"But you're not opposed to *having* sex, are you?" She kicks her sneakers off and climbs onto my lap with her knees outside of my legs and settles, wiggling her ass so my cock is lined up just right. "Oh, you're very hard."

My hands grip her hips, and I grind her against my zipper. I like this playful side of her. She's relaxed and not afraid to ask for what she wants. "Kiss me."

"Yes." Her soft lips glide back and forth across mine. Slowly, she tilts her head and pushes her tongue into my mouth.

I tug her blouse over her head and drop it on the couch. Then I break away, having to look at her. Her tits are full and perky, and I'm positive they're begging me to taste them. I lower my head and kiss the valley between them. She smells so damn good, and her skin is like silk under my tongue. I flick it across her nipple until it hardens, and then I switch to the other one.

I lean back and try to look confused. "Are you okay? You're breathing pretty hard."

It takes a second for her to get my tease. I breathe a sigh of relief when she chuckles.

"Since you're up for it, I think we should have wild Saturday morning sex and not worry about any dry cleaning."

"Well, if that's what you want," I say, laughing.

"Only if you're volunteering."

I'm speechless for a second. Her comeback makes my dick twitch. "I'm at your disposal." I pull her up onto her knees. "Stand up for me."

I strip her jeans off, and I'm panting at the sight of the tiny patch of silk covering her. I lean over and breathe in her scent. Musk and sweetness waft off her pussy, filling me with hunger. I pull her panties off and look at her for a minute.

"You're staring."

"I could look at you like this forever." I take off my shirt as I stand, unsnap my jeans, and take my underwear to the floor. My shoes stop me from kicking them across the room. "Damn. Hang on." I finally get my feet untangled and bare. "That was romantic."

She snickers. "It was fun to watch."

I stretch out on the couch. "Get over here and straddle me."

She smiles as she spreads her knees and settles her bare pussy over the length of my cock. She's so fucking beautiful when she gives in to her lust and allows it to take over her mind and body. I lean down and lash one of her breasts and then the other with the tip of my tongue. She makes a soft sound and leans down so I can worship her.

"You make me fucking crazy. I'm going to lick and suck on these beauties until you beg for release." I run two fingers through her folds and gather her juices. She watches as I spread that moisture over her nipples. "Then I'll do the same to this sweet pussy." I nip her just hard enough to hear her moan.

"Oh, God. That feels so good."

I chuckle while pulling as much breast into my mouth as possible, then switch to the other. I run my tongue over every inch of her creamy white skin. Her hips start moving, writhing, so I slip my hand down to her swollen lips and find her clit. She moans and grins against my fingers. I pull them back.

"No. Don't stop."

"Trust me." I pat my chest. "Come up here."

She slides up to my stomach. The heat and moisture against my belly almost causes me to lose it, but I'm not done with her yet. "Closer." I tap my lips with my finger.

Chapter 4

Chelsea

"Uh...you want me to sit on your face?"

"Yes. Surely, you've heard of this."

"In books, but...."

"Trust me on this."

"I'll feel vulnerable and self-conscious."

"You'll feel in charge. You'll direct my every movement. Give it a try."

I scooch up and sit on his chest, moaning when the curly hair on his chest rubs against my wet pussy. He takes my hips and pulls me to my knees again. "Keep coming to me until my head is between your thighs, then lean forward and put your hands on the couch arm. After that, lower your sweet pussy until you feel my mouth. You'll know what to do."

I'm getting wetter by the second, just talking about it, so I move as he's asked.

"Good girl," he mumbles, pulling me closer with his hands.

His eyes are hooded and full of lust as I lower myself. I can't pull my eyes off him as I grip the padded armrest. He flattens his tongue and licks me from front to back, pausing to circle over my clit.

"Oh, my God." I slowly rock my hips back and forth. All rational thought stops when he takes my clit in his mouth, sucks hard, and then laves it with the tip of his tongue. I lose the capacity to think. All I can do is follow the demands of my body. I sink lower and grind harder.

"You're the best thing I've ever tasted." His words are muffled, but I understand him. "I'm going to feast on you until you come."

My hands release the armrest and wrap around his head, my fingers digging in, moving him where I need him. He explores and licks again and again as if he's starving. As if he wants to consume me. I shift, and all of a sudden, his tongue is inside me, thrusting in time with my moves.

I feel my orgasm building, so I bear down on his beautiful face and grind my way to bliss. The skin on my body catches fire, and my body jerks uncontrollably. My pussy clenches and shudders, flooding my juices on him and in him. It comes in repeating waves until I'm so weak I'm near collapse.

"Oh, yes. Taylor, yes," I moan. I'm unaware if I'm saying the words or just thinking them.

He slides his hands under my arms and supports me until the explosions inside my body slowly fade. Then he mumbles something I can't understand. Mortification hits me. I panic and roll off him. "Are you okay? Breathe."

He's smiling like he just won the lottery. "I'm great. I'm happy your first time was with me."

"I'm so sorry. It didn't occur to me that you might need to breathe."

"I could've tapped out at any time. You were amazing." He pushes the hair stuck to my sweaty face over my shoulder. "So that you know, it's called queening."

I kiss his still-damp chest. "Sounds appropriate."

"If the male is on top—"

"Let me guess. It's called kinging."

"I knew you were smart."

We stay in place for a while. I was in his arms, half on him and half wedged between him and the back of the couch. He idly strokes my hair, occasionally running his fingers through it. I relax against the rise and fall of his chest. I've never felt so content and at peace after sex.

"I think my actions told the story, but that was amazing if you didn't notice. I've never had an orgasm that strong."

He kisses the top of my head. "If I have my way, it will be the first of many."

I shift my body, and my leg brushes over his very large, hard cock. Before I know what's happening, we're sitting up, and he's reaching for his jeans. He drags them closer, pulls a condom from his wallet, and then covers himself. As if I'm no heavier than a feather, he turns me so I'm on his lap facing away from him.

"This is new, too."

Taylor's already proven he's got skills, and I'm excited to see where this goes next.

His arms slide around me. One hand cups my breast, and the other moves between my legs. Then his fingers move over my clit, making me jump.

"Do we need to stop?"

"No. I'm not that tender."

"Lift up for me. Now lean back." He moves me to just the right angle, and I feel his cock at my entrance. "Relax and sink down on me."

I don't hesitate. The feel of him at this angle sends my hormones into overdrive. "You feel good inside me."

"You're like a warm oven."

I lift and slide down again. Taylor groans a low growl. I swear he grows larger with each thrust. He presses between my shoulder blades, leaning me forward, and I place my hands on his thighs and cry out. I didn't think I could do it again, but an orgasm rolled through me after just a few thrusts. "Taylor," is all I manage to utter.

His hands catch my hips and lift me a little. I push up as the first hard thrust slams inside me. He sets a frantic pace, pushing me forward and pounding inside me. When his growl sounds like a wild beast and his cock pulses inside me, I come again.

Then I fall back against his chest, and his strong arms wrap around me. We're both soaked with sweat, but I don't care.

"You're amazing." His breath skates across the top of my head. "Fucking amazing."

He stands, swings me into his arms, carries me upstairs to the bathroom, and turns on the shower. When the water is warm, he puts me on my feet inside the stall. Then he pulls the condom off, drops it in the garbage can, and steps in front of me.

"Did I mention *you're* amazing?"

"No more than a couple of times."

He reaches around me and grabs my body wash, pouring some into his hand. He spreads the creamy liquid over my breasts and starts bathing me.

I grin up at him. "Interesting place to start."

"One of my favorite parts of your body."

"That was another new thing for me."

"The position?"

"That too, but I've never come three times in a row before."

His eyes sparkle like the sun glinting off the ocean, and he puffs his chest out. "We'll beat that number next time. Trust me."

"I do."

He continues to soap me down, and I realize it's true. I *do* trust him.

He treats me as if I'm made of china while he washes every inch of my body. He drops down on one knee, puts my foot on his thigh, and lathers it before repeating the process for the other side. When he finishes, he leans forward, flattens his tongue, and slides it through my pussy.

Then he looks up at me with a twinkle in his eyes. "I'm done unless you want more."

My legs almost give out. "I'll always want more, but I must pick up my clothes from the cleaners."

He stands, gives me a soft kiss, and then opens the shower door. "Next time, then."

"Next time."

I dry off, then do the same to my hair while he washes. I can't help but watch through the clear glass doors. His arms are up, his fingers scrubbing his scalp. The white foam sluices down his back, and my hands itch to bathe him.

His head turns slightly. "See anything you like?"

I snap out of my lust-filled daze and answer. "I see *a lot* that I like."

His hand captures his dick and strokes it. "That's good to hear."

"You're killing me." I laugh off the fact that my juices are flowing, and if I don't finish my hair and dress, I'll get back in the shower with him.

Then the water stops running, and the door opens. "Hand me a towel?"

I grab one off the rack, hand it to him without looking, and hurry from the room. If I stay, I'm going to climb him like a tree.

His laughter follows me. We're so at ease together already. It's like we've known each other for a long time. I dress quickly because that revelation scares the hell out of me. I think we're comfortable, but there's no "we" or "us" in the word comfortable. We're still feeling our way around in the dark. Getting too involved with Taylor could be a big mistake.

"I can't remember where I left my cleaner's tag, so I'm going downstairs." I don't wait for his answer. It's a true statement. Even though I've used the same cleaner for years, the owner is unhappy if I don't have it. I dig through my handbag and find it crumpled in the bottom, under my sunglasses. "Found it!" I call out.

"Good deal."

I shriek and whirl to find Taylor wide-eyed and smiling, standing about six inches behind me. He throws his hands in the air.

"I'm sorry." He doesn't try to hide the laughter that bubbles up from him as he walks to the pile of clothes still on the floor from last night. "Now that I know you're skittish, I'll call out a warning next time."

"I'm not skittish," I say, even knowing he will call me on it. "You snuck up on me. What if I'd given you a black eye, and you had to explain that on your first day at work?"

He dresses before walking to me and pulling me into his arms. "I'd tell them I got it defending the honor of a beautiful woman." Then he turns me around, smacks me on the bottom, and walks to the door. "I'm starving."

"Me too." The swat surprises me, but I get he's being playful. I lead him into the hallway, dig the keys from my purse, and lock the door.

Taylor pushes the elevator call button. "Kayla used to live in this building too, didn't she?"

"Right down the hall. She's looking for somebody to take over her lease now that she's living with Nick."

"Is it the same size as yours?"

"Exactly." Having him as a neighbor could be either great or disastrous. "Are you thinking about renting it?"

We step into the elevator, and he takes my hand. "I would never do that to you."

"You're probably right." He's a smart guy, and he knows things could get sticky. "With all the guys tromping in and out of my apartment at all hours of the day and night, it gets pretty loud."

"You are an evil woman who doesn't lie very well."

We walk hand in hand through the lobby and to the parking lot. Taylor leads me to his car and gets me settled. I half expect him to buckle my seat belt for me, but he doesn't. He walks around the front and climbs in. I give him the directions, and then we're on our way. Our destination's only a few miles away, and we park in front.

I open my purse and look for my ticket. "Damn it."

"You can't find it?"

"I had it before we left. If I don't have it, the owner gets pissed off. Losing it is not a good thing."

"Are we dealing with a man or a woman?"

"A woman. Why?"

"Come on." He walks around, opens my door, and drags me out while I'm still digging. He pauses when we walk in the door. "I'll get your clothes," he says softly.

The woman behind the counter is expressionless until she sees Taylor flashing his white teeth with a big grin. "What's a lovely lady like you doing inside on this beautiful spring day?"

She breaks into a smile, patting her hair and straightening her blouse. "It is a shame, but duty calls."

"Hang on, I have the ticket right here."

"It's Coffman, isn't it?" she asks Taylor, not me.

"Yes. That's amazing that you remember names with as many customers as you must have."

"I try," she says, then scurries away, hitting the button that turns on the moving rack full of plastic-wrapped garments. She stops it at C and retrieves my clothes.

"Found it!" I exclaim as I slap my tag on the counter. Then I pulled out my credit card and paid her. "Thank you."

Taylor and I walk outside, me stunned and him grinning from ear to ear. "You can turn that crap on and off at will, can't you?"

"Family inheritance." He holds the door while I get seated, then leans in, kisses me, and carefully hangs my dry cleaning on a hook in the back. "It is a nice day. Let's pick up some food and find a park."

"I'd like that. There's one about a mile on the other side of my apartment. The flowers are blooming, and there's a Chicken Hut on the way. I jog down there sometimes."

"Is it safe?"

"It's a popular trail, and people are always there."

Taylor drives back toward my apartment. His hand drops on my bare knee. "I told you about my family, but you haven't mentioned yours. Tell me about them."

"They sound like yours, but they live too far for me to pop in on them. I have a younger sister. I'm older by six years, so we're not as close as I'd like. She's twenty and in college."

"How far is too far?"

"They have a bed and breakfast on Kauai."

"You were raised in Hawaii?"

"I wish. My parents moved there after they retired." I point ahead. "The chicken place is on the next block on the right.

My dad broke his back when an eighteen-wheeler truck driver ran a red light. He was in and out of rehab for a long time before accepting the use of a wheelchair or sometimes a walker. The transportation company's insurance offered a large sum, and my parents accepted. They didn't know that Dad would never have sued or asked for a settlement. He's not that kind of person. Then they sold everything and moved to a better climate."

Taylor goes through the drive-through, and we each order a meal. The car fills with the scent of fried chicken, making my mouth water.

"It's a good thing the park's on the next block. The smell of that food has my stomach growling."

Finding a table was an adventure because lots of people were out enjoying the nice weather. We see a spot under a shade tree and spread out our lunch. Neither of us speaks for a few minutes. I glance up, and he's watching me lick my fingers. My stomach does a flip-flop. The feelings that rush through my body are exhilarating and scary at the same time.

"You miss your parents?"

"I do. I haven't seen them in a few years, but we FaceTime often." I finish off the last bite of the biscuit and put my box back in the sack. "My parents are wonderful people. The life they lived before the accident was as close to poverty as you can get. We never lacked love or emotional support, though, and they raised two girls on minimum wages. It may sound selfish or superficial, but my career has been my main focus. I've worked long and hard for my future."

Taylor wipes his mouth with a paper napkin, tosses his box in the bag with mine, and carries it to the trash barrel. Then he sits across from me with his hand extended—the warmth from his skin seeps into me.

"I don't think your goals and dreams are selfish. I respect them. They're a lot like mine."

"I hadn't thought of that, but you're right."

"Come on. Let's get you home. I have a stack of information and research to read tonight."

We hold hands again while we walk back to the car. He releases me when he opens the door for me. The drive to my apartment only takes a few minutes, and he parks in a visitor slot.

"You don't have to walk me to the elevator. I'm good."

"I know you are," he says, opening his door and coming around to my side. "I'm walking you to your apartment door."

Once inside and in the elevator, he wraps his arms around me. "I don't know what my schedule will be like coming up, but I don't want to distance myself too far from you. If that's acceptable."

The doors swish open, and I wait until we're at my door to answer. "I'd like that a lot."

He pulls me up on my toes, and his lips cover mine. What starts as a gentle meeting of our mouths morphs into a battle of tongues. We're both breathing hard when we separate.

He's laughing, still holding me against him. "Keys."

"I can't reach them."

"Right." Taylor steps back, and my hands tremble as I dig them out. Then I open the door and turn back to him. "Are you going to call me?"

"Count on it." He backs to the wall behind him and watches me close the door.

My knees are weak, my heart is pounding, and I'm grinning from ear to ear. I stumble to the couch and plop down. Maybe I'll sit here for a minute in case he comes back.

Chapter 5

Taylor

I sit on my couch, thumbing through a financial report for the second time. This job I start the day after tomorrow is important, and I need to concentrate. The Tate account is small in comparison to what Zack's company manages, but it's one that I've been assigned to manage and grow. It's important as fuck to me. So why can't I concentrate?

I grab my cell and send a text.

Miss me yet?
Who is this? LOL
Santa.
Cool. Do you have a present for me?
Damn right. I have something I'd like to give you.
You having a hard time concentrating on your paperwork?
Yup! Reading every paragraph at least twice.
Am I the reason you can't concentrate?
Absolutely. I need to see you soon.
Ditto. Go back to work. I'm turning in early.
Having a wild Saturday night like me?
Yes. The highlight was laying out clean underwear for tomorrow.
Groan. Have dirty dreams of me.
Of course.

I glance at my cell. It's eleven o'clock. Time has got away from me. I stand and stretch, then adjust my hard cock. *How does Chelsea not have a man in her life?* I shake that thought off, put my work back into folders, and go to bed. Tomorrow's Sunday, and I can catch up on my reading in the morning. I climb between the sheets, shove a couple of pillows against the headboard, prop myself up, and then turn on the small television that sits on the chest of drawers. There's an old movie on, and I try to numb my brain with things other than work and Chelsea Coffman.

***

I wake with my head lolled to the side, my neck aching, and I see the Sunday morning news on television. I grab the remote and turn it off. Rolling out of bed, I head to the kitchen and start the coffee pot. While I wait for a hit of caffeine, I take a shower, shave, and brush my teeth. Then I pull on my underwear, return to the kitchen, and fill a huge mug with wakeup juice.

I'm seriously interested in the paperwork Zack gave me to look over. I'm determined to go to work with every piece of information I can absorb, so I log onto my laptop and research the holdings and investments of the Tate account. I want to make this client money. The sooner, the better.

At some point in the day, I also need to organize my wardrobe for work. It's vastly different than the stuff I wore in college. I've filled out the forms for HR and damn near memorized the reports, all while trying not to think of how badly I want Chelsea sitting next to me.

I pick up my phone and call her.

"Hello there."

"Hey." I can't help but notice she sounds like she's just finished a marathon. "Am I interrupting something?"

"No, silly. Hang on for a second."

I hear a male voice telling her, "thank you."

"I forgot my water bottle at home and was about to die of thirst."

So, she's out for a run, which is more than I've done. "What are you doing for dinner?"

"If you can beat a BLT sandwich and a movie on Netflix, I'm interested."

"How about the steak in town?"

"God, I don't remember the last steak I had."

"Then I'll make reservations and pick you up at seven."

"I'd like that."

"See you soon."

I spend the rest of the day rereading the details of a couple of Zack's accounts for which I'll be joining meetings. Then I change into jogging shorts, a T-shirt, and running shoes. Spring weather can be iffy, so I take advantage of the day and head toward the school.

The closer I get to the campus, the older I feel. Maybe I should give up my apartment. I'm sure somebody would be glad to be this close to the college. At twenty-eight, I look more like a professor than a student. My stomach growls, reminding me I skipped lunch. I turn and head back home while thinking about seeing Chelsea in a couple of hours.

I'm not showing up at her apartment starving, so I take the steps two at a time, finishing my run sweaty as hell. Once I get inside, I go straight to the kitchen, which my mom would describe as too small to turn around, grab a frozen dinner from the freezer, and pop it in the microwave. This mode of cooking has been a big part of my life for years and is one of the reasons I run. Then, I pull a bottled iced tea from the fridge and wait for the timer to sound. Standing at the counter, I polish off my turkey dinner with green beans and corn. It isn't the most nutritious food, but it does the job.

Next, I strip and go to the bathroom. Turning the water to medium, I drop my clothes in the hamper and step under the spray. My mind immediately goes to Chelsea. I get hard just thinking about her naked body. I lather up, rinse off, and cradle my cock in the palm of my hand. The image of her riding my face and the sounds she made has me gripping myself and jackhammering until I shoot streams of cum against the tiles.

Then I clean up my mess, dry off, shave, and head to the closet, where I pull out a pair of black slacks and a white shirt. After looking in the mirror, I exit my townhouse and enter my garage. After getting in and starting the car, I back out and wonder if she's ever been to Silken. Since her two best friends are very much into the BDSM lifestyle, I have to believe she knows enough about it not to be frightened by it.

Her apartment is on the opposite side of town from me, so I take the ramp and join the traffic on the expressway. The experiences I had while in Europe couldn't be described as "dates" by any stretch. Tonight will be the first time in a long time I've picked up a woman at her door and taken her to dinner. I catch myself driving too fast in anticipation.

I knock on her door at precisely 6:30. She opens it and takes my breath away. Her hair is pulled back and up in a loose bun, or whatever it's called. She's wearing a black skirt that stops a couple of inches above her knees and hugs her body in all the right places without giving away too much. Her blouse shifts as she steps aside to allow me to pass. It's almost the same green as her eyes and looks to be made of silk. Her heels make her a few inches taller.

"Hello, gorgeous."

"Thank you. You clean up pretty well yourself."

I step into the room, closing the door behind me. My hands grip her arms and pull her closer until her breasts brush against my chest. I lean down and run the tip of my tongue across the seam of her mouth.

Her hand slides up my chest, and she smiles. *Jesus, she feels good, like she belongs in my arms.* I kiss her, envisioning all the filthy things I thought of doing to her after I left yesterday—and all day today. My lips muffle her soft moan, and her free hand reaches down and cups my cock through my slacks.

"I wouldn't do that if you want to make our reservation."

She grins up at me. "Can you be fast?"

Laughing and talking at the same time, I turn her toward the couch. "Bend over the arm and hold on tight."

She whirls and does as I ask. I don't pause. I shove my slacks to the floor while she wiggles out of her skirt and pushes it and her panties down on top of my stuff. I grab a condom from my pocket, cover myself, and then take hold of her hips. I slide my cock back and forth over her pussy until she's wet and ready.

Then I slam home.

"Oh, Taylor. I've needed this all day. Fuck me."

Her words set me on fire, and I demonstrate what she does to me at a rapid pace. I piston my hips hard and fast, sliding my hand around to her clit and working it diligently. I'm ready to blow when she suddenly speaks.

"I'm coming, Taylor!"

My name comes out of her mouth in long syllables.

Her pussy clamps down as if trying to hold me inside. I explode right behind her. Then I drop forward, resting my hands next to hers, keeping my weight off her. "You are amazing."

"So are you."

"Stay right where you are." I hustle to the bathroom, wet a washcloth, and bring it back to wash her gently. "Let me help you dress."

"I got it." She puts on her panties and then slides up her skirt. Her hands go to her hair. "How do I look?"

"Freshly fucked and beautiful."

"Perfect. We need to hurry."

We left her apartment, and she locked the door behind us. When the elevator deposited us on the ground floor, we ran to my car. We're both laughing. I waste no time getting on the expressway and pushing the speed limit.

Chelsea starts singing along with the radio. She surprises me with a beautiful voice.

I turn it down to hear her better, and she stops. "Keep singing. Please."

Her tone is perfect, and her range is amazing. A popular song comes on, and she sings along with it. "Have you ever considered a career as an entertainer?"

"Oh, no. My throat closes just thinking about singing in front of a crowd. Besides, I'm happy right where I am."

"We haven't talked about your job. Tell me what you do."

"I'm the administrative assistant to the VP of Accounting at Slater Advertising. I spent a few years as the human resources director's administrator. I worked hard hours paying my dues, but it's paid off. When Morgan married Zack and resigned, I was promoted to her vacant slot."

"I can tell by your tone of voice that you're happy there. I hope I can say the same in a few years."

"I'm betting you excel and climb the ladder quickly. According to Morgan, she's been asking Zack to turn the reins over to someone else so he can concentrate on managing the club."

I take the exit ramp, leaving the traffic behind and staying on the access road until we reach Bavette's parking lot. I stop in front of the valet service stand. "What time is it?"

"We're ten minutes late."

Employees open both our doors, and we meet at the hood. "We should be fine."

She slips her hand inside my arm and gently grasps my bicep. "I'll have a tantrum if they say we're too late. Maybe that will change their minds."

I look down at her, and her eyes have that sparkle that's a dead giveaway. "You really are evil. Behave so I won't have to punish you later."

The door swings open before I can reach for it. We're welcomed and seated without any fuss. She's silent as she goes over the menu, flipping the pages back and forth. A frown appears on her beautiful face.

"What's wrong?"

"Did you see the prices? *That's* what's wrong. This place is too expensive."

She's worried about me. Every time she opens her mouth, I respect her more. "It's okay. Zack gave me a nice sign-on bonus."

"Oh. Good for Zack."

"I'll spend some of it on clothes, but tonight is about having a nice dinner with you. Deal?"

"Deal."

We order wine and then salads and ribeye steaks. Hers medium rare, mine rare, and baked potatoes for both of us. After the server leaves, I lean back in my chair. I still have questions about her family. "Do you stay in touch with your folks much?"

"Once a week, Mom and I FaceTime." Her eyes light up. "Even if we don't have any news, we still check-in. My sister and I talk occasionally, but Daphne's wrapped up with her college studies, friends, and, no doubt, parties."

"What about your dad?"

"He changed after the accident. I think pain can alter anyone's personality. We talk if Mom sticks the phone in his face. He tries to chat, and I know he loves me, but his hate for being in that wheelchair has taken away all his humor."

Then our dinner is served, and the steaks are perfection. Watching Chelsea enjoy hers makes every bite I taste even better.

"OMG." She swallows a morsel. "It just melts in your mouth. I can't remember the last time I ate beef, except for hamburgers and tacos."

"I'll make sure we improve your intake of red meat."

And I will. I want to take her to the best places. I pour her a third glass of wine when we finish eating. She licks her lips before taking a sip, and my cock reacts. I've held myself to one glass since I was driving, but there's no reason for her not to enjoy herself.

"I have a question about something you said earlier."

"Ask away."

"You threatened to punish me if I was rude. Exactly what were you planning to do?"

"There was no threat issued. It was just a *warning*." I'm glad she's brought it up, but I'm not sure we should discuss it after she's had those three glasses. "If you're ready, I should get you home. We both have to be at work tomorrow."

"You're probably right. I can't show up with dark circles under my eyes. I might be getting another promotion."

"That's great." I nod at our server, and she brings the check right away. I drop cash in the leather folder, stand, and pull Chelsea's chair back. Then I rest my hand on her back, absorbing her warmth, and escort her to the valet station. I hand over the ticket, and the young man disappears into the parking garage.

"You can answer my question on the way to my apartment."

"I wasn't planning on discussing it until you're sober."

She steps away and looks up at me. "If you think three glasses of wine affected me, you're wrong. I can't tell you why, but alcohol doesn't hit me like it does other people. I don't get hangovers, either."

"Where have you been hiding all my life?" I laugh just as my car stops at the curb. Once we're both settled, I turn the car toward her place.

"Harrumph." She clears her throat, reminding me of the unanswered question.

"There are many ways to punish, but first, the punishment should fit the crime. Spanking a bare bottom, denying orgasms, lashes with a whip, isolation, and more. It has to be something both parties agree to, and that's the best way to correct a sub."

I hold my hand up, hoping to keep her from talking. To my surprise, she remains silent. "I was not in any way suggesting you're my sub or even want to be. It was more of a joke."

"A joke, or were you testing my reaction?"

"Maybe a little of both." She's quiet, leaving me to wonder if she will never want to see me again or if she'll surprise me and be interested. She twists in the seat a little, turning to look at me in the face. I take a quick glance at her but can't read her expression. "Do you have anything else you'd like to ask me?"

"Not that I can think of right this minute. I learned a lot when Morgan searched the internet for information on Doms and subs and BDSM before she started dating Zack. She shared articles and blogs written by women who have been involved with the lifestyle in various stages for years. Next, it was Kayla digging around online. She even found a few women who were slaves. I know for sure I will never be anybody's slave. That's not open for discussion."

"I'm glad because it feels like we click. Maybe we met in another life or something."

She turns in her seat and stares forward.

I reach over and place my hand on her thigh. "You were the first person I thought about when I returned to the States."

"Why? Because Morgan and Kayla are in the lifestyle, and since I'm their friend, I'll fall in line?"

My jaws clamp down so hard my teeth hurt. *Is that what she thinks of me?*

"What the fuck kind of question is that? *Fall in line?* I don't give a damn who your friends are, how they live, or who they fucking live with."

"Then why?"

Thank God we're at her apartment. I park in a visitor's space and turn off the engine. "After I started visiting the different BDSM clubs in Europe and developed a better understanding of it, I knew that I wanted and needed to have it here. You were the only woman who came to mind. Other than that, I don't fucking know why." I get out and go open the door for Chelsea. "I'll take you upstairs."

We walk silently from the car, through the lobby, up in the elevator, and to her door. She makes no effort to get her keys out. Instead, she looks up at me.

"It wasn't my intent to insult you or make you angry. Are you dumping me now? If so, say it."

"That decision is solely yours. I think I've made it clear that I want you like crazy. Let me know what you decide."

Then I lean down, kiss her forehead, turn, and walk away.

"Taylor?"

I stop and turn around slowly. She's walking toward me, so I wait. "Chelsea?"

"What punishment would you give me for disrespecting you?" She shifts from one foot to the other. "I'm just curious."

I look down, and her hand is on my chest and over my heart. "I'd spank your pretty little ass."

She has that evil sparkle in her eyes again. "Hard?"

"If it's appropriate." I hold out my hand and issue a command. "Give me your keys."

She digs in her purse and then hands them to me.

"That's the door key."

I hoist her up until she's draped over my shoulder, ass pointing forward. She squeals and kicks, but she's not putting any real effort into it. I unlock the door, carry her inside, smack her butt, and then stand her in front of the couch.

Her eyes are wide, revealing her dilated pupils. She's unsure what will happen, but my gut tells me she's up for it. I toss her keys onto the coffee table, then unbutton her blouse and remove her bra, barely able to drag my gaze away from her perfect tits. Her skirt goes next, along with her shoes. I leave the little slip of material she calls a thong. Then my hands scale her satiny skin from her feet to her waist. "You are so beautiful."

"So are you."

I sit on her couch, drag her across my lap, and run my hands over her perfectly curved bottom. She's kicking and laughing again.

I smack her naked ass. Once on each cheek. Not hard, but enough to leave a pink handprint.

Then I massage her ass to ease any discomfort.

She turns her face up toward me. "Is that the best you've got?"

"You're a cheeky woman, aren't you?" I smack her butt hard enough for it to sting and give her five on each cheek. She's wiggling across my legs and groin. I know she can feel my hard-on pushing against her stomach.

"Are you going to stop now?" she asks.

"That's not the way this works. *I* decide when to stop." I give her two more on each side, stop, and return to massaging the pink skin. She moans. I slide my hand under her and seek out her sweet spot. I wet my fingers in her juices and rub a circle around her clit. "I think the spanking turned you on."

"I'll never tell."

"You don't have to. Your pussy says it all." I lift her so she's straddling me. Before I can say anything else, she starts undoing my belt and then unzips my pants.

"Give me a condom."

"Say, please."

"Please give me a condom so you can fuck me silly before you leave."

"Take off your thong." I pull it sideways, threatening to rip it off.

She scrambles away and makes quick work of dropping it to the floor.

"I don't know when we'll see each other again, with you at your new job and me vying for the promotion. Tonight might have to last us awhile."

While she's talking, I'm doing what she asked, and by the time I'm covered, she's crawling back over my thighs. I grasp her hips and lift her onto my cock. She's sopping wet, making it easy for me to thrust home. "Is this what you want?"

"Oh, my God. *Yes.*"

I pull her head down, and when her mouth meets mine, I claim her hard and fast. My mouth, my cock, and my hands are prepared to give her something to remember. My fingers dig into the soft tissue of her breasts. Not enough to bring her pain, but enough to elicit a moan from her. She lifts up and meets me as I drive deep inside her over and over. I take her hand and tuck it between her legs.

"Play with your clit."

Her head tilts back, away from my lips. Then she spreads her folds and starts rubbing. *Oh, fuck.* The view is almost the end of everything, but I gather myself and enjoy watching as my cock moves in and out of her. I've never seen anything so erotic. My chest tightens at how beautiful she is helping me pleasure her.

"Taylor," she says with a gasp.

Her pussy clenches my cock as if she's going to hold me inside of her warmth forever. "Come for me. I'm right here with you."

I grip her hips and hold her in place while I pound into her heat some more. Her entire body jerks and her mouth opens, but I can't understand a word she utters. I pull her down as jets of cum explode into the condom. With every spasm of her tight pussy, I come harder.

Chelsea collapses against my chest. Her face is buried against my neck. We're both soaked. My hands go around her, and I stroke her back. We stay here, content, breathing hard but not caring. Then she laughs. I feel it more than I hear it until she pushes upright.

She smiles up at me. Her cheeks and chest are flushed, and her nipples are still semi-erect.

I capture both of them with my fingers. "I guess we'll have to do this again sometime."

We look at each other for a long minute. I love the satisfied look in her eyes. Her lids are getting heavy, so I slide her off my lap and stand.

"Soon, I hope."

"Stay put."

"Woof. Woof."

As I walk into the bathroom, I laugh at her attempt to bark like a dog. I remove the condom and dispose of it in the trash can. Then, I run warm water over a washcloth and carry it to the living room. She's rolled over on her back. "Woof?"

"I heard you laughing."

"Spread your legs."

She flops her knees open, and my cock twitches. It's a sight I'll never get over. I kneel and gently clean her. "You like me taking care of you?"

"I could get used to it."

"Good, because I like how at ease and relaxed you are with me." I return to the bathroom and take care of myself before going back to the living room to dress. By the time I'm finished, she's pulled a throw over herself. I scoop her into my arms and carry her to bed. Then I jerk the covers back and lay her down.

"Thank you."

I kiss her on the forehead. "I'm gone. Have a good day tomorrow."

"Hmm. You too."

I start for the door and turn back. "Sorry, but you need to lock up behind me."

"There's a keychain on a hook next to the breakfast bar. Take either one of the silver keys."

Then she tucks her hands under her chin and falls asleep, looking like an angel.

I move quietly, take one of the keys, leave her apartment, and lock the deadbolt. It means a lot that she trusts me enough to give me total access to her life.

Chapter 6

Chelsea

Over the past few months, Taylor and his lunchtime texts have been the highlight of my workday. Even if we don't see each other daily, we talk on the phone every night. He's submerged himself in just about every account at Pierce Brokerage. I don't know whether Zack is pushing him or if he's determined to prove himself. The good news is, he's promised me he's soon going to cut back on the hours he spends at work.

It's been a few minutes since his last text, so I push back from my desk, stick my head in the open door, and tell my boss I will pick up lunch. He gave me his order, and I went to the elevator. Baker's sub shop is right around the corner and is always busy at this time of day, so I fall in line and wait my turn. Then my cell dings, telling me I've received a text. It's interesting how my heart speeds up when I see it's from Taylor.

How's your day going?
Great. Did you clear your schedule for the weekend?
I sure did.
Miss you.
You have no idea.
Gotta order lunch. See you tonight?
Count on it.

It would be so easy to get attached to Taylor, but I am trying hard not to expect too much. I've tried to keep him from my thoughts, but so far haven't been successful. The memory of his hands on my body is imprinted on my brain. My nipples react just as if his mouth's on them.

"Excuse me." A stranger taps my shoulder. "I think they're calling your number."

"Oh, thank you." I grab the two sacks and hurry away. I don't easily blush, but my cheeks are hot.

I collect myself while I walk back to the office. Acting like a silly girl with a crush isn't my style. I catch the elevator and walk to my boss's office. I tap on the doorframe, and he nods. His back is to me, and his phone is against his ear, so I place the sack in the spot he likes and then turn to leave.

"Chelsea."

His tone stops me in my tracks. I turn and look at his grim expression. His lips are drawn into a thin line, and his eyebrows are drawn together. My mind is racing. *Have I done something wrong and typed up a report full of mistakes?* My thoughts have wandered a little over the past few months since Taylor has become a part of my life, but I can't believe I'm in trouble.

"What's wrong? Should I close the door?"

He nods and waves his hand to one of the chairs across from his massive mahogany desk. "I understand," he says to the person on the phone, then drops it into its cradle.

I swallow hard. I have never been in trouble in my five years with this company, so it has to be something else. "Has something happened to my family?"

"No. Nothing like that. I was going to wait until you'd eaten, but I figured you'd want to know immediately. You're not getting your promotion."

After waiting months for them to decide, confusion clouded my thoughts. "But I haven't even been interviewed yet."

"I know. If it helps, I recommended you highly."

"Thank you." I don't want him to think I wanted the job to escape him. "It's disappointing, but I knew some other people here wanted the position, too. May I ask who got the job?"

He opens his mouth but pauses as if searching for the right words. "I understand it's the president's niece."

I hold my head high and blink back my surprise. "Okay. No worries. I'll get over it. Besides, I like working for you."

He holds out his hand to stop me from talking. "That's not all. The announcement will be made in the next few days, but I wanted to tell you myself. I'll be retiring as soon as a replacement can be found."

I've been perched on the edge of my seat, but learning of his retirement is such a shock that I slump back into the chair. "Is it too nosey of me to ask why? You're still young."

His tight facial expression finally relaxes. He sighs and half-smiles. "Not at all. I'm sixty-plus, and it's time to enjoy what's left of my life. My wife and I are moving into a retirement community in Florida, where we'll enjoy the golf cart social life."

"Then I'm happy for you."

He nods and opens the sack, holding his sandwich. "Thanks. Go eat your lunch and then finish that report. We still have work to do."

I stand and walk out of his office. Instead of eating in the break room with my co-workers, I sneak into an empty conference room and give in to my disappointment. I turn a chair around, facing the city's skyline, and sit watching the world go by while I battle against tears. I have worked hard, stayed late, and taken work home, and I am determined to claim a position of worth. It's disheartening, but there will be other opportunities.

My cell buzzes, and the caller is Taylor. He texts but never usually calls me at work.

Maybe he has a sixth sense and knows I need to hear his voice.

"Hey," I say as cheerfully as I can muster.

"Hey, yourself. How about I pick up some food and a bottle of wine? No cooking for you tonight."

The tight band around my chest eases a little. The warmth in his voice restores my inner balance. "That's a fine idea."

"Chelsea? Baby, what's wrong?"

"Nothing, really. Will you get out of there in time to get dinner? I can pick up something."

"Not necessary. I can be at your place by seven."

"I'm dying to hear all about your day."

"Great. See you then."

"See you," I say, smiling as I disconnect.

Then I turn the chair back to the conference table, open my sack, and eat lunch. Knowing Taylor's bringing dinner tonight buoys my spirits. I stand and stride back to my desk. The sadness and surprise of the news are still with me, but now it's mainly because my boss is retiring.

I finished the report and put it on his desk. He nods but is already engrossed in a brochure for a retirement community. I slip silently from his office, finish my work, schedule his appointments for tomorrow, and email them to him.

"Chelsea!" he calls.

I grab my iPad, walk into his office, and sit across from him. "Sir?"

"You caught up for the day?"

"Yes, sir. What can I do for you?"

"Go home. And close my door behind you."

I can't help but smile. "Okay. Was that all you needed?"

"Yes. See you in the morning."

"Absolutely."

I shut down my computer, grab my purse, and hurry out of the building. The minute I sit behind the steering wheel of my car, a thought hits me: *I don't remember the last time I left work early, but I know exactly where I'm going.*

I pull my cell from my purse, call my doctor, and text Taylor.

Off work early. Called my doctor's office. I'm on birth control, so I'm going to have blood drawn. I hate condoms. Do you want to do the same?

Fucking right, I do. You're brilliant. I'll go tomorrow at lunch.

About you picking up dinner, don't. I'm cooking.

If you're sure...

I'm sure.

I look up the address for the lab and drive straight to it.

Am I being presumptuous?

Absolutely. But he didn't hesitate, and I want to see where our relationship goes.

I park and go inside the tiny office in a strip mall. The clinic isn't busy; only two people are ahead of me. I grab a clipboard, fill out the attached form, return it to the counter, and pay for the test. When my name is called, blood is drawn, and ten minutes later, I'm back on the road.

I think traffic is light, but remember being ahead of rush hour. The trip through the grocery store is quick, and after I park at home, I get out and carry the two bags of groceries to the elevator. I'm in a great mood now. I've shaken off the day's disappointments and look forward to seeing Taylor. Odd, since we were together just last night.

Maybe I should tell him to bring some clothes and leave them in my closet?

I park and make my way up to my apartment. While I inserted the silver key to unlock the dead bolt on my door, I remember telling him he could have one for himself. And he took it. That in itself sends chills rushing through my body.

I carry the grocery bags to the kitchen, empty them, and then line each item on the counter in order of how I'll use them to make my mom's spaghetti. The sauce needs to cook for a while, so I go upstairs and change. I kick off my shoes and put them in the closet. The rest goes in the hamper. Then I grab a pair of shorts and an old T-shirt.

It's old because I've been called a messy cook.

Getting started isn't hard. I chop the onions and open a couple of cans of tomato sauce and one of paste. Now I'm in business. Measuring and stirring the six different spices into the liquid fills my kitchen with memories of home. When the sauce starts bubbling, I turn down the heat, cover the pan, and hit the stairs again.

A nice hot shower is next. I strip again, turn on the water, and slide under the spray. Lathered, I pay special attention to all the parts of my body that Taylor might be interested in after dinner. After I've finished and dried, I let the girls swing free but put on a sexy thong, a blue pair of yoga pants, and a matching pullover.

After getting the bed made, I head back down the stairs again. I stop at the bottom and think how lovely a ranch-style house would be without stairs.

With time to kill, I call Morgan and Kayla for a FaceTime conference chat.

Morgan starts talking before I can speak. "You and Taylor are getting pretty tight. Are you planning on coming to Silken anytime soon?"

"I don't know. We're getting to know each other first."

"Fuck me," Kayla says with a laugh. "He's been lusting after you for a long time. At least tell him you want to check out the club."

"Okay, so I've got a question. I need to know if you are honestly happy with your situation. I know you're both crazy in love, but if you could, would you change Zack or Nick into the men you *thought* you'd spend the rest of your lives with?"

I receive two quick shakes of the head. "No way. It's freeing for me. Zack knows and respects my boundaries. He respects me. Anything we do is because that's what we both want."

"Same here." Kayla leans closer to her cell. Her eyes narrow. "Has Taylor forced you to do something you didn't want? Hurt you in any way?"

"No," I answer quickly. "You don't need to threaten to cut off his balls like you did Zack."

"I said I'd do it if he hurt Morgan. The same goes for Taylor." Her eyes are twinkling and full of humor.

"I'll warn him."

"You do that."

We laugh, and I check the time. "I have to go. My spaghetti sauce needs attention. I love you guys."

We end the call with promises that we'll get together soon. I return to the kitchen, pull out a knife, get the Italian sausage cut up and crumbled, then add it. After I fill a large pan with water, I settle on the couch to read a couple of blogs the girls had sent me links to.

A knock on my door stops me. I close my laptop and walk over to look through the peephole. Then I unlock and open it. "You're early."

"Zack escorted me out."

I step back and let Taylor pass. "Fired already?"

He hands me a bottle of wine and picks me up by the waist, bringing me eye to eye with him. I wrap my legs around him, push the door closed with my foot, and give him a quick kiss.

"Not yet. Zack thinks I'll burn out if I try to absorb everything at once."

I open my mouth to speak, but Taylor's lips descend instead, cutting off any words or thoughts I might have. He's kissing me like we haven't seen each other in days.

"Something other than you smells delicious." He carries me to the kitchen, hovers over the sauce, and takes a deep breath. "I can't remember the last time somebody cooked for me."

"All I need to do is throw the pasta in boiling water and put the bread in the oven. Twenty minutes, tops."

"That's cutting it close." He cups his hands under the swell of my ass. "I'll wait for dessert."

"You'll have to put me down if you're going to open the bottle of wine."

He slides me down his body. "That's an unfair choice."

"The opener is in the top drawer," I say while turning on the water and filling the pan for the pasta. Once it's on the stove and the burner is on high, I take the bread from the sack, slice it, and get it ready for the oven. "You're very cheerful. Today must have gone well."

"It went by so quickly, I can't say whether it was good or not. Zack was right, sending me home with the rest of the office. My mind was on overload."

He pours two glasses of wine, placing one next to me, and then sets the bottle on the table.

"Dishes and silverware." Again, I indicate where he can find them. He turns sideways and slides past me, brushing against my ass. My skin heats when he stops long enough to nip the tip of my earlobe. His good mood is contagious. Before I realize it, the pasta is ready.

I put everything in separate bowls and lay them on the table so he can add as much or as little as he wants to his plate.

"I can't believe I'm so hungry." Taylor holds my chair as soon as the food is on the table, then sits directly across from me. He lifts his wine glass. "Thank you for this. I'm sure you had a busy day, too."

"It was interesting. Eat. Serve yourself." I touch his glass with mine and sip the delicious nectar. "This is excellent."

He piles enough food on his plate for two people, then digs in. His moan tells me he's enjoying his meal.

"The bread!" I exclaim. "I forgot to put it in the oven."

I started to rise, but he caught my hand. "This is perfect. There's no need for bread."

We make small talk while we eat. I love watching him. He's relishing every bite as if a great chef had prepared it for him. Then my cell plays a ringtone I recognize. "I'd better get that. It's my mom, but she usually calls on Wednesday."

I grab my phone off the counter, sit back down, and accept the FaceTime call. "Mom? Is everything all right?"

"Oh, honey. I didn't mean to worry you. I'm calling to tell you I won't call Wednesday." She laughs. "I could have texted, but I wanted to see your face."

"I'm glad you did. What's up?"

"The manager we hired has worked out great. So well that your dad and I are going on vacation."

"Who leaves Hawaii to go on vacation?" Taylor asks softly.

"You have company?" Mom's hearing was always great, and it still is.

"I do." This is opening a conversation I don't want to have yet.

Taylor smiles, stands, and walks around behind me. Then he drops to his knees and smiles at my mom. "Chelsea makes the best spaghetti sauce I've ever had. Why do I think she learned that at your elbow?"

My mom is now absolutely beaming at him. "I like to think she learned to cook from me."

"She also inherited her looks from you."

"Mom," I interrupt, elbowing him out of the picture. "Where are you and dad going?"

Her cheeks are bright pink, and I can't stop the smile spreading across my face.

"We did the ancestry thing, and Dad decided we have to go to Germany, Switzerland, and Austria to see how many Coffmans we can locate."

I'm thrilled they're going to travel, but with Dad's back, I worry. "Is he physically up to it?"

"He's enthusiastic enough to use that wheelchair less and less. He just needed some incentive. We signed up for a fourteen-day tour." She leans closer to her phone. "I won't worry so much about you now that I've met your new man. He's very handsome." She's whispering like he can't hear.

I glance at Taylor, who's carrying our dirty dishes to the kitchen. "Slow down, Mom."

"I'll take good care of her!" he calls out. He's enjoying this too much.

"I'll send pictures."

No doubt, she's already daydreaming about a wedding and three grandkids.

"Oh, wait. Any news on the promotion?"

"I didn't get it, but I'm fine with it."

"I'm so sorry."

"Don't be. Go see lots of castle ruins in Germany. Have a wonderful time."

"Love you," Mom says, using her upbeat tone.

"I love you, too. Kiss Dad for me."

I end the call, stand, and take the leftovers to the breakfast bar, where Taylor is leaning back with a big grin on his face.

"You really do look like her."

"She's a mother with two single daughters. One look at you, and suddenly, she's having wedding invitations printed."

"That's just the way moms are." Taylor leans around me. His hands rest on my shoulders. "Tell me about the promotion."

"It's just one of those things. You really don't want to hear about it, do you?"

"Of course I do. Talk to me."

We finish cleaning up the kitchen, working in tandem, me washing while I repeat the double dose of bad news I've had today. Taylor listens intently while he dries, then puts away the dishes and pans. He sounds genuinely interested. I take the dish towel from him and hang it over the oven door. "I don't know why I didn't use the dishwasher."

"It was more fun this way. And it also gave me a reason to rub against you when I moved from one cabinet to another."

"You do realize my kitchen has ample room for two people?"

"I hadn't noticed." Then he backs me against the counter. "I'm sorry about your promotion. Sounds like your president isn't very smart. Maybe he's a sugar daddy to this *niece* he's hiring."

I chuckle at that idea. "That would run the rumor mill at top speed."

"It's their loss for not giving you the job. Fuck 'em."

"I hate that my boss is leaving the company, too, but I understand his desire to spend more time with his wife."

Taylor catches my hands and turns me into him. "I'm sorry."

"Thank you. I'm not going to stress about it."

His hand slides under my hair at the nape of my neck, his thumb stroking the pulsing vein in my throat. "I should go home and let you get some rest, but I haven't had dessert yet."

I remember how happy Kayla and Morgan were today. Neither has second thoughts or regrets about accepting Zack's and Nick's lifestyle preferences. I slide past Taylor, pour another glass of wine, and carry them to the couch. Then I pat the cushion next to me. "We need to talk."

His eyes widen. "That's the one sentence I never want to hear from you." He joins me in the living room and takes his glass, but he doesn't sit beside me. "Maybe I should stand."

"What? Why?" It hits me that I've misled him. "You can't see my laptop screen from there." I open the page to the blog I've been reading. "I can't do a show-and-tell with you over there."

His stance relaxes as he rolls his shoulders. "You confused me. Who feeds a guy a dinner like that and then cuts him loose?"

"I just realized how that sounded. I'm sorry." I pat the cushion next to me again. "Please."

He sits close, our thighs touching. I place the computer on his lap and watch his face closely. His expression doesn't change, but his eyes are focused on the page. He scrolls down and finishes reading.

"You've been researching." He places my computer on the table.

"Morgan, Kayla and I FaceTimed earlier today. I asked them if they would change how they live if they could. Neither would. They love their lives just as they are."

"The more you know and understand, the easier it is to decide. There's no one set way to live the BDSM lifestyle." He wraps his hand around my ponytail and kisses me. Not passionately, but softly. "You wanted to talk?"

"It's more of a request." It occurs to me that I'm not nervous or frightened in the least. "Will you take me to Club Silken this weekend?"

"If that's what you want."

"Right now, I want *this*." I motion between us with my hand. "When I'm with you, there's nothing or no one but us. My mind and body yield control to you."

His mouth suddenly slams into mine, his tongue sweeping inside, possessing me. His lips are hard and demanding as he consumes me, and I relinquish all control to him. When he finally leans back and studies my face, I understand we've entered a new relationship phase.

Chapter 7

I look into her eyes and see honesty, questions, and trust. "We'll go hang out, take a tour, or watch a few scenes, whatever you're comfortable doing."

"Do I need to fill out paperwork first? I remember Morgan having to decide what her likes and dislikes were."

Blood rushes to my cock at Chelsea's words. The need to touch her and feel her body against mine is so strong I pull her across my lap. She rests her head on my shoulder, and I stroke her back.

"I'll check tomorrow, but yes, we'll have a code of conduct to agree to. You'll have to identify what you're interested in and what you're not." I bury my nose in her hair and let the sweet citrus aroma fill my lungs. "I don't have to join the club right away."

She tilts her head up at me. "I hadn't thought of that. It's costly."

"Not to worry. I know the owners."

I bend my head and cover her lips with mine. What starts as tender quickly morphs into a hard and fast kiss.

I stand with her in my arms. Concern that I might be pushing her runs through my mind. I carry her up the stairs, place her on the bed, and dig a condom from my wallet before I sit beside her. "Are we going too fast?"

"I don't feel like we are. Truth be told, I feel like I've known you for a long time. For the first few weeks after we shared that long, hot stare, it was your face I conjured up when I pleasured myself."

I laugh and nod. "Same, except mine lasted longer than a couple weeks." I unbutton my shirt, kick off my shoes, and shove my slacks and underwear to the floor. My cock is standing at attention and pointing at my navel.

"You are so beautiful." She looks up at me after staring at my erection. "And huge."

She climbs off the bed and drops to her knees. Her small hand wraps around me, and she licks me from the base to the tip. My dick expands and twitches while she strokes me, lowering me in line with her mouth. She laps me with her tongue, swirling it around me for a few seconds. Her gaze comes up and meets mine just as she opens her delicate mouth and slides me inside. I'm struck speechless. She has this way of making love to my cock. My legs almost give out. I toss the condom on the bed to free both hands.

"You feel so good. Your mouth is like nothing I've ever felt before." I push my hands onto hers and guide her deeper. Her fingernails dig into my ass as she opens her throat. I lose it, fucking her mouth as if I'll never get the chance to do it again. Pressure builds, sending warning shots. I release her hair and grab hold of her shoulders. "Stop. It will be too late in a second."

She shakes her head and relaxes her jaw, sliding all the way to my base. She moans, sending vibrations to my balls, and I try again to pull back, but her nails dig in. I roar as streams of cum fill her mouth and jettison down her throat. Then I lean forward, placing a little of my weight on her shoulders as she swallows every drop and then licks me clean. She's been watching me all this time, and her eyes are sparkling like the stars in the sky.

She's smiling when she stands. "I love watching you come."

"There are no words to describe what just happened. I'll remember this night for as long as I live." I take her hand and sit her on the bed. "I can't seem to wipe this silly smile off my face."

"It was something I wanted to do." Her face is glowing pink, so I stretch out on the bed and hold my hand out to her.

"Come up here." I tap my fingers on my lips, and she immediately starts scooting up my body. Her scent of arousal reaches my nose, and I breathe deeply.

She pauses.

"Don't stop. Come ride my tongue."

She immediately starts scooting up my body until her knees are on either side of my head, and I'm staring at her wet pussy.

"This is a first for me."

"I promise to stop if you don't like it."

She drops down, and I pull her clit into my mouth. She tastes so fucking good I lick and suck, soaking my face with her juices. I'm the happiest bastard on earth. She pushes down and grinds hard. Her fast orgasm catches us both off guard. Leaning forward, she puts her hands on the wall and lifts, but I'm not finished with her. I pull her back to me and drink from her until every last drop of her juice is in my mouth. I'll never get tired of her taste.

"Holy shit, that was quick." She grins as she slides off me like melted butter onto her back. "That was amazing. Having you come in my mouth had me so aroused my orgasm took me by surprise."

"I'm available anytime," I say, pushing into a sitting position and holding my hands out to her. "Come straddle me."

She glances at my erect cock. "Oh. We most definitely have to take care of that."

"Wrap your legs around me." I look around and locate the condom I'd thrown on the bed earlier. She slides both legs around my hips. "This is called the Lotus position."

"I like being close and face-to-face."

I grab the condom, rip it open, and slowly roll it over my cock. She takes the packet and tosses it to the side. I slide into her in one stroke and pull her tightly against me. I cover her lips and sweep my tongue inside while at the same time grinding against her.

She closes her eyes and wraps her arms around me as our bodies move in sync, combining speed and pressure into one action. I release her mouth. "Look at me."

"Taylor," she whispers. "I didn't believe I could come again so fast, but..." Her words trail off as her pussy clamps down on me. "I'm going to do it again!"

"Yes. Again," I demand.

Her body shakes, her legs tighten around me, and her eyes glaze as she shudders. "Oh. My. God."

She begins to quiver around me, and with a loud groan, I follow her over the edge. We cling to each other while she milks the last drop of cum from me.

Neither of us moves or speaks for a few minutes, and I wonder about this connection we've formed. She's like a flower blooming in my hand. Open, willing, honest, and funny, and mine.

Mine for now.

Finally, Chelsea makes the first move. She leans back and places kisses all over my face. Then she laughs. "Nobody told me sex could be addictive."

I laugh with her. "That may be the nicest thing you've said to me."

She slides off me and flops onto her back. "I'm not sure I can move."

"Then don't." I get up, go to the bathroom, dispose of the condom, and clean myself up. I wet a fresh washcloth with warm water and take it to the bedroom. She's relaxed with a soft smile, yet she watches me as I clean her. When I'm finished, I lean down and press a kiss to the top of her pussy. "I hate to kiss and run, but I need to get out of here and let you get some rest."

She lifts an eyebrow at my joke. Then she gets up, fishes a long T-shirt from a drawer, and pulls it over her head. "Staying up late tonight was worth it."

"Damn right, it was." I put on my clothes, then sit on the edge of the bed to slip on my socks and shoes. She drops to her knees, takes my loafers from me, and slides them on my feet.

"Thank you. You're full of surprises tonight." I take her hand, and together, we stand and walk downstairs to the door. "Does Friday or Saturday work best for you?" I smooth my fingers down her long, soft hair and marvel at how beautiful she is and how lucky I am.

"Saturday. But if you're so inclined to see me, I'll be here Friday night, too."

I lean down and place my forehead against hers. "I'll be in touch long before then."

Then I kiss her soft, luscious lips and walk out the door.

****

I lean back in my chair, realizing that getting off work early this past Monday had been a luxury. It's been balls to the wall since I walked through the door Tuesday morning. The wife of one of the firm's main clients filed for divorce, and all hell broke loose. The guy had called almost every hour, demanding we figure out how to keep his wife's attorney from obtaining the value of his investments. I told Mr. Bankston there was no way to prevent it since the subpoena had been delivered first thing Tuesday morning, and it set him off. He got furious and called Zack.

Bankston's call resulted in a meeting with Zack and me, and then he told the greedy bastard the same thing I had. Our wealthy client spent the rest of the week threatening to sever all ties with Pierce Brokerage.

I stand and walk to Zack's office to let him know I'm leaving. He sees me and waves me inside.

"Come in. Have a drink."

"Thanks." I step inside and take a chair across from his desk.

"Your first week has been a baptism of fire, but I can't promise it won't happen again." He pours a shot into a crystal glass and hands it to me. "You handled Craig Bankston brilliantly."

"That last session was tense. Bankston is so full of resentment and anger at his wife and her attorney that he's thinking with his emotions. I wasn't sure if you'd be pleased."

"You can't let clients bully you. If I'd been concerned, I would have delicately intervened."

I take another sip of Zack's expensive whiskey. "Bankston was at a crossroad, and he made the right choice."

"Well, I was impressed and appreciate every hour you put in this week." Zack takes a sip and leans back in his chair. "Are you and Chelsea coming to the club Saturday night?"

"She hasn't changed her mind yet, so yes. I think she's excited about it. It was her idea."

"So I heard. Morgan and Kayla have shared a lot of what to expect with her. I don't think they got into exact details, but those three tell each other almost everything."

"I figured, and I like that she has close friends. They're important to her." I sense Zack has something he wants to add, so I ask the question. "Any advice?"

"Don't fuck it up." He laughs and then leans forward. "Every couple is different. Talk, talk, talk. If you two don't communicate, your relationship will suffer."

"I'll make sure we discuss everything."

"Last thing to remember. There's a chance Chels will decide against being a sub, whether at home or the club. If that happens, you'll have to choose between the lifestyle and her."

"I hope that doesn't happen." I throw back the shot and stand. "But I get what you're saying. Thanks for the drink and advice."

"Morgan and I will be there to welcome you two, but Chelsea may be uncomfortable with that. If so, we'll disappear. Now get out of here. Have a good weekend!"

"You too." I leave his office and walk to the elevator. It *has* been a great first week. I'd gone on instinct when I called Bankston's bluff to move his portfolio elsewhere. And I'd asked him who he thought would help him rebuild his portfolio better than Pierce Brokerage.

Now, I'm tired and energized at the same time. My steps are light as I walk to my car. I hope Chelsea isn't upset that my hurried phone calls and texts have been brief all week.

Once I slide behind the wheel, I realize I can't wait to hear her voice. I miss her upbeat personality, sassy mouth, soft skin, warm heart, and open mind. I start the engine, blast the air conditioning, and turn down the radio. I tap the word *mine* on my cell and lean back in the seat.

"Taylor." Her voice makes me smile.

"The one and only. How's my girl?"

"Good. I just talked with my mom. The flight was long, but any discomfort had been forgotten because of their excitement. The hotel they're staying at tonight is super-nice, and they met a couple their age to pal around with."

"I bet they'll have an amazing time. Any more excitement at your job?"

"Lots of office buzz about my boss's early retirement and who will replace him. Pretty dull stuff."

"Are you up to me bringing dinner by your place? I've missed the hell out of you."

"That's the best news I've had this week. How about I order delivery, and you come straight here."

"I'm backing out of my parking spot right now."

"Drive safely."

"I will." I smile as I leave the garage and weave my way downtown to the expressway. I can't remember the last time someone asked me to drive safely. That Chelsea did wipe away the last residuals of exhaustion I'd felt as I left work.

Traffic is typical for Friday at quitting time, but the stop-and-go doesn't get under my skin. Not when I know what's at the end of my drive.

Chapter 8

Chelsea

At his knock, I unlock the door and wrap myself around Taylor. He's holding a folder in one hand, but I can handle just one of his arms. "It's okay if you use the door key. I wouldn't have told you to take it if I didn't trust you."

His kiss is soft and sexy as his lips touch and release mine a couple of times. Then he lowers his forehead and rests against mine.

"Damn, I missed your face."

"Good, because I missed yours, too. This week took forever to be over. What's in the folder?"

"A couple of pages for you to look over and fill out."

I take the folder from him and put it on the coffee table. "Yay! We're getting ready for tomorrow night?"

He nods. "We can talk about your preferences tonight if you want."

"I want *you*." I step back and allow my gaze to slowly slide from the top of his head to the shiny shoes on his feet. Wearing a dark gray suit and a red-and-gray striped tie, he's the perfect example of what a male model looks like. I reach up, loosen the knot, and release him from his neck bondage. Unbuttoning the top two buttons of his shirt, I nod my approval. "You are too handsome for your own good."

He takes my hand and leads me to the couch, pulling me onto his lap. "What does that mean?"

"I'm betting that more than one woman who works at Pierce Brokerage has been trying to see what's hiding behind your zipper."

His eyes open wider, and he laughs. I love the sound because it comes from a place deep in his chest and goes all the way to his eyes.

"Not one woman looked at me this week. Well, Caroline Hayden was with me a lot."

"What do you mean? Who's she?"

He's teasing. It's written all over his face. He doesn't know that Morgan has previously mentioned Mrs. Hayden. She is sixty-five and has been Zack's assistant forever. She's referred to as his work wife.

His chest puffs out, and his hand slides up and down my back. "Are you jealous?"

"She's a little too old for you, right?" Then I hop off his lap and go to the kitchen. "Dinner's getting cold."

I grab a couple of paper plates in one hand and our pizza box in the other. Then I feel him. He's so close behind me that the faint smell of his cologne mingles with the Italian spices. His breathing ruffles the hair on top of my head. There's a need I can't describe that builds inside me when he's this close. "Are you hungry?" I choke out.

"You have no idea," he whispers, pushing closer until our bodies touch.

I swallow. "Will you get a couple of beers from the fridge and bring them to the table?"

His hands lightly skim my waist, then slide under the bottom of my shirt. He strokes my bare stomach up to just under my bra. "Of course."

"Thanks."

He moves away, leaving my nerves a jangled mess. And he knows it. He gets the two cans, pops the tops, and carries them to the table. "Are you coming?"

I walk over and spread out our dinner before his pun hits me. I sit across from him, slide my hand under the back of my blouse, unhook my bra, then drag the straps off my shoulders. With one pull, I remove the bra and toss it onto an empty chair.

"Not yet."

"Touché." He adds a slice of pizza to my plate and then takes two for himself. "I missed talking with you this week. Did things settle down at work?"

"The rumor mill dried up today when the president's niece came in to do her paperwork for human resources. She starts Monday." I take a bite and almost sigh. I love Italian food.

"Everyone got a look at her?"

"Yep. She looks just like him."

Taylor chuckled. "A lesson in not listening to gossip."

"Absolutely. She seems sweet, and according to a friend in human resources, she has some experience."

"What about your boss?"

"I don't expect a change right away. The interview process should start soon if they don't promote from within." I slide a third slice onto Taylor's plate and clean off the table. "Want another beer?"

"No thanks." He stands and brings his empty plate to the trash. Leaning against the breakfast bar, he eats and watches my every move.

"What's on your mind?" I ask.

"He runs his hand through his hair. I got my blood test back. Did you?"

"Yes. I can't believe I forgot to tell you. I'm glad the results came before our night at Silken."

"Are you nervous about tomorrow night? Scared?"

My heart melts at his concern and the serious look on his face. "No, and I won't be as long as you're with me." Then I put my hand on my hip. "Are *you* scared?"

His eyebrow lifts. "Not as long as you're with me."

"That's not an answer."

Three long strides, and then he's standing toe to toe with me. He looks down at me with those blue eyes that change to the color of stormy clouds when he's aroused. He pulls off my blouse and then removes my shorts and panties. His fingers skim across my nipples, ribcage, and belly, stopping just short of where I want him most.

"You have too many clothes on," I protest.

"You don't get to make that decision." He turns me around and pulls me snug against his chest. "Now close your eyes."

I lower my eyelids and relax into him. He covers them with something soft and ties it to the back of my head. Then he leads me from the kitchen to the living room. Holding my elbows, he turns me around and pushes me until I feel the couch against my thighs.

"This is the first time I've ever been blindfolded."

"No talking, and do not touch me." With one finger in the middle of my chest, he pushes me onto the couch. "I want you to experience what happens to you without seeing or touching. Just *feel* what's happening."

I nod vigorously. Goose bumps race up my arms, and I'm breathing hard. His hands grip my hips, pulling me to the edge of the couch. I lean back, wondering what happens next.

"Spread your legs."

I do as he says. He takes my hands and places them at my sides. My breathing sounds loud in the silence of the room. His footsteps tell me he's moving away from me. The fridge opens and closes.

Then silence.

I strain to hear movement.

Is he watching me while I anticipate his touch? I rest my head on the couch, showing him I'm unafraid.

His tongue is warm and damp when he slides it over my nipple. Then he pulls it into his mouth, teasing it until it's rigid. I whine and arch my back when he abruptly releases it with a pop and moves away. Something cold circles my nipple, and a flush of adrenaline floods my body. The sensation of icy heat sends a shiver of pain and pleasure through me. "Oh my God."

"I said no talking." His mouth covers my frigid nipple with wet warmth while what has to be an ice cube moves to my other breast. I'm ultra-aware of every nerve ending, and I ache for more.

My body shivers and twists as the ice slides down my chest, around my navel, followed by Taylor's tongue. Stopping at my mound, both leave my body. Inside my head, I'm picturing myself levitating in search of his touch.

When his fingers separate the folds of my pussy, I almost cry with relief. He gathers my juices and rubs them on and around my clit, then rapidly licks it off. My skin is on fire. I lift my hips in a silent plea for more, but he moves away.

I cry out when the ice slides back and forth over my soaked pussy. Then my breath catches as it slides deep inside me.

"Taylor!" I call out his name. My blood runs south, and I'm suddenly lightheaded.

"Fuck, you're so hot inside, the ice is already melting." His tongue stabs deep inside me and imitates the movement of his cock.

I squirm and lift my hips. "Please. Make me come."

The sound of his zipper almost makes me come right then. I spread my legs even wider and waited for his touch.

And wait.

"You are so beautiful. I was going to make you wait until tomorrow night to come, but I can't do it. I need to be inside you now."

His strong hands turn me so I'm on my back. He catches one of my legs and rests it over his shoulder. The head of his bare cock slides back and forth between my lips, getting wet with my juices. I tilt my hips, and he sinks slowly inside my body. His skin is hot as he fills me, stretching me to accommodate him. Then he stops moving. "You feel unbelievable without a condom. Warm and soft."

He pulls almost completely out before sliding deep again. There's no frantic pounding of the flesh. We're gliding, relishing the intimacy we're sharing with each thrust. Every time I spasm, I flood him with the fluid my body releases. My nerve endings are live currents of electricity, and the blindfold magnifies all my body's sensations.

"Oh. Oh." I lift my hip as high as I can. "It's too much. Too good. I'm going to come."

His mouth covers mine, and I kiss him back. I moan as he slowly re-enters me. Sinking deep, he moves in a slow, steady rhythm and reawakens my senses. As the tempo picks up, I head for the cliff again.

I will hold back. *I will.*

"Come. I need to feel you come on my bare cock." His thumb finds my clit as his thrusts get faster and harder until his hips are crashing into me. "Come now!" he demands.

I explode. I'm trying to call his name, but the roar of waves in my head pulls me under. My body convulses, clenching him, and then I slowly come down.

"Feel me come. I'm going to fill you with my cum." His hips jackhammer into me until he slams home and holds me still while he pumps stream after stream deep inside me. The noise he makes is somewhere between a growl and a shout as he keeps pounding until my body reacts and I come again. Then he slides off the blindfold and stares into my eyes. He props himself on one elbow, leans down, and kisses me.

I blink a couple of times and then smile up at him. I cup his cheek in my hand. "I had no idea."

"About?"

"How much more intimate and personal sex would be without a condom." I can't tell him my heart is so full it's about to burst. "Best sex ever."

"Ever." He nods, and his eyes sparkle. "I'm glad the first time you had no-condom sex was with me."

Every bone in my body is liquid. It's not exhaustion but complete peace. I realize his cum is slowly trickling out of me. "So am I. I'm glad you're the only one."

He lifts my leg off his shoulder. Glancing down between my thighs, he smiles and runs his finger through our combined cum. "I wish you could see what I see."

"Ah, but I can feel it."

"I'll get a washcloth."

My apartment is quiet except for the sound of running water. I stretch my arms over my head and relax. Contentment rushes through me. Again, I feel like a kitten ready to curl up in a ball and sleep. The wet, warm terrycloth against my bare skin brings me back. "Thank you."

He slides a towel between me and my leather couch. "Lift your hips."

"If anyone had told me that someday I would be this open and comfortable with my body and sexuality, I would have laughed. You've taught me so much; tomorrow night, you'll teach me even more."

****

Chelsea

Sunlight on my face brings me out of a deep sleep. I barely remember Taylor tucking me into bed and then leaving. I was totally and completely satiated when he left. I roll over, pick up my cell, and hold it above my face. *Crap*. I sit up. I never sleep this late on the weekend. I have things to do. I slide out of bed and walk to the bathroom, stopping in front of the mirror to study the woman looking back at me. Who wakes up smiling like a lovesick fool? Okay, it's not love, but I'm deep into liking Taylor Horne.

I shower and dress in yoga gear before starting my weekend duties. I pull back the drapes in the living room and let in the sun. I'm super energized this morning, and soon, I have the sheets changed and the floors cleaned. Even both bathrooms shine.

Satisfied I've earned a break, I fix a giant mug of coffee and a bowl of cereal, grab the folder, and carry it to the living room. I'm smiling again as I park my butt in the exact same place Taylor placed the towel last night. I'm a few hours away from my afternoon appointments, so I relax on the couch.

Then my cell buzzes, and I see Morgan's checking in.

"Hey, woman," I greet her.

"Hey, yourself. Are you decent and receiving guests?"

"That's a yes to both questions. Come on over."

"Good. Kayla and I are downstairs."

"Wow. This is becoming a routine. I like it. See you in a sec."

I should have expected them since today's the big day.

I unlock the door and wait in the hall for them. Those two never show up empty-handed, and this morning is no different. Kayla is carrying a bag of pastries, and Morgan has a travel tote and dry cleaner's bag.

They peck me on the cheek as they pass me. Morgan goes upstairs, and Kayla heads straight to the dining room table. I see Morgan's brought me club dresses to borrow.

"We didn't bring coffee this time," Kayla says, spreading out napkins and divvying the sweets. "I'm so hungry my stomach thinks my throat's been cut."

I spring into action and fix a fresh pot.

Morgan bounces down the stairs, stops at the table, and stares at Kayla. "What the hell did you say about your throat being cut?"

Kayla places her bear claw on a napkin and licks her fingers. "If I have to explain it, you won't get it. Think about it."

I arrange cups, sugar, cream, and the pot onto a tray and carry it to the table.

Morgan helps me empty the tray. "When will you buy one of those fancy coffee makers?"

"Never. I like the one I have." I can't wait any longer to ask about the clothes she carried upstairs. "So, you brought me one of your dresses for tonight?"

"I brought a few for you to choose from." Morgan winks at me. "You're going to knock him on his ass."

"OMG! We're just going as observers tonight."

Morgan finishes her cream cheese roll. "That's what I thought, too, when I first went. But before the night ended, we walked down a deserted aisle and watched a couple in one of the scene rooms. I was so turned on that Zack got me off right where we stood."

"And we're just hearing about this now?" Kayla leans forward with both elbows on the table. "Tell us more."

"That's more than you need to know." Morgan turns to me. "Let's go to your bedroom, and you can try on the outfits and choose the one you like best."

Kayla stands first. "I didn't bring you anything. You're put together better than me."

"No way, you've got way bigger boobs." I stand and start up the stairs. "We don't have long. I have a couple of clean-up, fix-up, and paint-up appointments this afternoon."

Morgan chuckles and follows me. "It's just one of the things we do for our men. Especially for a big night."

"And sometime before Taylor picks me up, I have to finish my like and dislike page."

"All I can say is keep an open mind." Kayla kicks off her shoes and crawls onto my bed to watch me try on the outfits. "There are things on that questionnaire I thought I would never try. Boy, I was wrong."

"You both will be there, right?"

"Yes, but we're not staying. You don't need to worry about us hanging around tonight."

Chapter 9

Taylor

I step off the elevator before the doors open all the way. The last time I spoke with Chelsea, she was leaving to have her nails and toes done, plus whatever else she had planned. She was bubbling, and her excitement was contagious.

I know Morgan and Kayla had stopped by to check on Chelsea, and I'm sure they gave her all kinds of advice.

I decided to use my key as she suggested. The lock turns quickly, and I open the door slightly. "Honey, I'm home!" I call out.

"I'll be down in a minute."

I close the door and walk over to the window. Unlike my place, which looks out over the busy street below, her view of the pool area is great. It's quiet in her apartment, and I'm comfortable here.

"I'm ready."

I didn't hear her come down the stairs, and I quickly turned around. My lungs empty every bit of air they hold. I must look like a complete idiot as I step toward her.

"Say something. You're scaring me." She waves a hand in front of her body. "You think it's too much? Too little?"

A chill races down my spine. "I've never seen anyone so beautiful."

"Really?"

"You take my breath away."

I don't walk any closer. It's not because I don't want to touch her. It's because she's stunning, and I want to soak this moment in. I want to take a mental snapshot of how beautiful she looks and place the memory in the recesses of my mind for safekeeping.

Her long hair is loose in the back, with each side braided, pulling it away from her face accentuating her graceful neck. Her shoulders and arms are bare, and a black corset tucks in her already tiny waist. It also cups her breasts, pushing them higher, and her nipples are barely covered with a small slice of silky black material. Her hips and ass are covered with the same skin-hugging fabric. Her legs are bare and shapelier than ever from the high heels on her shoes. I run my hand over the lower half of my face just in case there's drool on me.

She did all this for me.

She blinks quickly a couple of times. "You shaved your scruff."

"I did. I feel naked without it. I'll leave it off until I'm established at work or rich and famous. Whichever comes first."

She takes one step toward me. "I like you with or without."

"Come here," I say in a firm tone.

She strolls toward me, her hips swaying with each step. She stops a foot from me, puts her hands behind her back, and lowers her head. I catch her chin, pulling her up so she can see my eyes. My fingers slide over the soft swells of flesh the corset has put on display.

"Morgan brought me some of her outfits to borrow, but I'd already bought this one. It doesn't leave much to the imagination."

"It means I'm going to kill every male in the club who even looks at you."

"I wasn't sure you'd want me to go this far. Do you want me to change into one of the other outfits?"

"Oh, hell no. I'm so very proud of you for doing this for me." I hold my hand out, and she places hers in mine. She's flushed and happy that I'm pleased. And I am so fucking humbled by her bravery.

"I want to kiss you so fucking badly, but I'm afraid we won't leave this apartment if I do. I do have one question, though. Are you wearing panties?"

"I am. I bought a pair at the dress shop. Morgan said Zack loved them so much he bought her a dozen of each color." Her hand drops to the hem of her dress. "Do you want to see? They're so cool."

"Stop." I adjust my aching cock, searching for a comfortable position but not finding one. "I can't take much more."

"Then we'd better go." She turns and walks to the couch, picks up a black cape, and swirls it over her shoulders. Then she handed me a small wallet and the forms she filled out after I left last night. "That's got ID, just in case I need it."

I tuck it into my hip pocket and hold onto the papers. Then I open the door and watch her stroll through. "Even wearing the cape, you look hot as hell."

She tugs it tighter around her body. "I'm going to be a wreck. I should change into something less revealing."

"Stop that." I lock the dead bolt, slide the key into my pocket, and take her hand. "You're adorable when you're nervous."

"Then I'm going to be adorable all night."

She looks back and forth down the hall while we make our way to the elevator. Luckily, there's no one around, and we don't have to share on the way down. I wrap my arm around her shoulder, holding her closely when we leave the building and step to the curb. Our driver, Gabriel, hops out of the limo and opens the door for us. "Good evening."

"You're taking me in style."

"I am. My lady deserves a fancy carriage." I help her inside, turn and wink at Gabriel, and slide in beside her. "Either that, or I've stolen a limousine." I lean over her, buckle her in, and kiss her before taking my seat. I'm trying to get her to relax, but I'm not sure it's working. "It's okay. I know the owners."

Gabriel slides behind the wheel and turns to face Chelsea. "So, you're the third part of the Morgan-Kayla team. I'm Gabriel Thorne, chief of security for all three of the co-owned clubs. Your safety is top priority for the security team and me. In the club, you'll notice monitors walking around wearing red vests. They're also there for your safety. And don't hesitate to speak up if you need help." He passes a clipboard back to me. "Chelsea, did you read, sign, and bring the copy of Club Silken's rules and expected behavior policy?"

"I have it." I attach them to the clipboard.

He removed it and handed her preference sheet back to me. "That's between you two."

Chelsea leans forward. "It's a treat to meet you. I've heard nothing but praise about you from Morgan and Kayla."

"I've heard the same about you. If this scoundrel doesn't treat you right, you come find me." Gabriel winks at me, then pushes a button, and the black divider glass slowly rises.

"You know him well?"

"Define 'well.' I think he's a great guy, but Gabriel has never mentioned a personal life to me. We talk about work, life, and the weather, but never family. I'm not sure anyone but Zack knows him really well. I know that Gabriel doesn't socialize or participate in the club with the guys. Now that he's in charge of all security, he only drives the bosses or people they deem important."

"What about your paperwork?"

"Zack gave me mine at work. There's no preference page for a Dom. That is strictly so I'll know more about your desires. I unhook my seat belt and move so I'm facing her. "Show me those panties you're so proud of."

"I knew you were dying to see," she says, grinning from ear to ear. "I've been waiting for you to ask."

She lifts her bottom slightly and shimmies her skirt up to her waist. "Good thing this material stretches."

"Spread your legs."

She releases her seat belt, slips down, and opens wide. My entire body goes on alert. The small, black satin patch between her legs has narrow straps holding them on her. I move to the floor of the limo and kneel between her knees. Then I run my fingers around the outside of the piece of cloth covering her bare pussy. "So soft and smooth."

"I thought you were interested in my underwear."

I lean forward and breathe deeply, allowing her scent to penetrate my brain. "I got sidetracked." I pull that little patch to the side and run my tongue through her slit. "You taste so good."

"Let me help."

My hand cups her warm flesh. "Baby, you can't make this any better."

"Watch." Her hands slide down the straps running over her hipbones, stopping at a small rose on each side. With the flick of her hand, the thong has come apart. "Handy, don't you think?"

"It's genius." I carefully pull it down and lay the satin strip of material on the limo seat. My fingers spread her outer lips open. "I could look at you all day."

I dive into her heat before she can speak.

"Oh God." Her hips lift up, giving me better access. "Please don't stop."

I don't know how much time I have, so I slide a finger inside her and pull her clit into my mouth, working her hard. Her hand grips the back of my head, and her thighs clamp down on me, crushing my ears into my skull. Her body shakes, and I know she's close. I use my thumb to breach her tight asshole. Her mouth opens into a silent scream while her pussy clenches and releases my finger. I could watch her come forever. She gives everything to me, holding back nothing. I take her into my arms, pulling her onto my lap.

Her body is still twitching in the afterglow. "You make me come so hard. I'm sorry if I almost smothered you."

"If I died buried in your pussy, I wouldn't care. And you'd have one hell of a tale to tell." I open the compartment where the wipes are stored and clean her gently. "We're probably getting close to Silken. We better get you back into your panties."

"Why? You'll just take them off later."

"You don't get to question why I want something done tonight. You just do it." I glare at her for a moment. "Besides, it will be fun to rip them off."

"This Dom/sub night should be interesting."

I glance out the window and see nothing but trees and shrubs. "We're on the main road to the club. It's hidden off the highway and is a private drive."

"So we're close?"

I nod. "We're going in as observers, but we should discuss your list." I picked it up from the limo floor where it was dropped earlier. I scan it and try not to show my surprise. "I love that you're open to trying anything except whips, but are you sure about this? You didn't mark a hard no on anything else."

Chelsea secures her thong and gets her shirt back in place. "I want to experience life. Try new things. Learn what I like and don't, and I want to do it with you. Besides, isn't that what the color red is for?"

"If you say 'red,' everything stops. The scene is over. We'll dress, leave, and then discuss where we go from there."

"Okay, I understand. I'll be one hundred percent sure before I use that word."

"Do you want to scene tonight?"

She's looking down at her fingernails. "Can I wait and decide later?"

"Of course. But if we do, your role as my sub starts tonight."

The limo comes to a stop in front of the club. I fold her list, slip it into my pocket, and open the door before Gabriel gets to us.

"I'll see you inside." He turns his back and walks up the stairs, entering and closing the doors behind him.

I extend my hand to Chelsea, and she exits with the grace of a queen. She's going to take this club by storm. "Let's get you inside and put a bracelet on you." I take her hand in mine.

"I get a white one, right?"

"Yes, you do." I love that she can look like a sexy siren one minute and an excited girl on her way to her senior prom the next. "You should lose the cape."

She bites her lower lip and then nods. We leave it in the limo.

Then we enter the outer doors and stop at a desk where the guard who works the entrance is sitting behind a table. Gabriel is standing right behind him, holding a bracelet.

"If you give me your hand, I'll slip this on your wrist, and you're good to go."

Chelsea steps closer and watches as the plain band slides over her hand. She smiles at him, and I swear this bull of a man blushes. "Thank you."

Gabriel swings the inner doors open and stands aside. "Relax and enjoy. You're as safe as you were in your mama's arms."

"Ready?" I ask her.

"I am."

I rest my hand on her back as we walk inside Club Silken for the first time. It's nine o'clock on the dot, exactly when Zack expects us.

A long bar is to our left, and the stools are full of couples and a few single men. The dance floor is to our right, and Chelsea pauses to watch. The music is soft and sexy. I don't recognize the song, but the beat is perfect for the few bodies barely moving. Some people are fully clothed, but a few are in various stages of undress. Another's partner is backed up against his chest, and he's running his fingers through her pussy. Another couple has the woman's breasts on display, and her partner is feasting on a nipple.

Chelsea looks up at me. Her pupils are dilated, and her mouth has formed into a silent *oh*. The man glances at us and says something to his partner, and they both smile while looking straight at Chelsea.

"I may have to ask one of the monitors to stay with us. Men *and* women are already drooling over you."

Her gaze slides back to the dance floor. "Can we just walk freely around the club?"

"Everywhere except the new addition that's referred to as the dungeon. It's designed for Doms and subs who live the sadomasochistic lifestyle."

"We won't go in there, right?"

"No. That's not my style, nor yours."

"Good. I trust you."

"As you should." I take her hand and lead her to an area where some tables and booths are tucked away, but there are also a few out in the open. "Zack and Morgan are waiting for us in one of the larger booths."

"Let's find them. I need a drink."

Then Zack walks into view and starts toward us. He stops when Morgan speeds past him.

"She looks like a queen," Chelsea says as she walks away from me to meet her friend.

I laugh at her description. Queens wear bright colors, but probably not in the fashion Morgan does. Her outfit is red spandex. A narrow band covers her breasts, and a second does the same from her belly button to the tops of her thighs. The look is made spectacular by a long overskirt that's open in the front. It's full and swirls around her legs as she slides across the floor in spiked heels.

I glance at Zack, and he smiles while shaking his head. We both start moving and join our women.

"Welcome to Silken." He leans in and kisses Chelsea on the cheek before shaking my hand. "Let's get you two settled with a drink."

Once seated in a circular booth, Chelsea looks around at the other couples. Her gaze lingers on two women kneeling on the floor of a booth while two men are having drinks.

"Where are Kayla and Nick?"

"They won't be here until around nine-thirty. They're scheduled to scene on the stage at eleven. Nick has become quite the expert with the cat-o'-nine-tails, and they've agreed to give a demonstration."

A tall redhead wearing a long, skintight dress comes to the table to get our drink orders. Zack introduces her as Danielle Moore, the club manager. She shakes my hand and fawns over Chelsea. Danielle admires Chelsea's club dress, her hair, and then her choice of friends.

Chelsea is silent until we're alone with Zack and Morgan. "I distinctly remember Kayla saying that nobody would ever whip her. She was quite colorful about what would happen to the guy who tried."

Morgan smiles and snuggles closer to Zack. "I don't doubt her reaction would be violent if it were done in anger, but she's so relaxed with Nick. She learned through watching others and experimenting with Nick until she found something she liked."

Chelsea sips her wine and swirls it around in the glass. "So, he does it because she wants him to?"

"And it pleases him to make her happy." Zack reaches around Morgan's shoulders and pulls her close against him. "Why don't you two walk around and watch a few or all the open scenes? Nobody will object to you watching. If they did, they would be in one of our private rooms with the door closed."

"I'd like that," Chelsea says.

I slide out of the booth and help her do the same. "Thank you for inviting us as your guests. We'll try not to embarrass you." I wink at Zack.

Chelsea wiggles her fingers at Morgan and then starts tugging at her skirt. I catch her hand in mine. "You are perfect, and you look beautiful."

Morgan pins me with a stare. "Take care of my girl."

"Every second of my life."

Chapter 10

Chelsea

All the research I've done and the talks I've had with friends and Taylor don't fully prepare me for how my hormones react inside Silken. With his hand on my back, the heat searing my skin through the corset I'm wearing, we take our first steps into the world where Taylor wants to live.

Had he just told Morgan he would care for me for the rest of his life?

After thirty years together, my father's eyes still light up when Mom walks into a room, and she reacts to him the same way. I want a love like that.

I stumble, and Taylor's strong arm steadies me. I glance up, and his gaze is locked on mine. His eyes sparkle as if I'm the only woman in the world. My chest tightens as my heart swells.

We return to the dance floor and then turn down an aisle. This section is laid out much like an open-office area. There's ample room to move around, yet clear dividers keep each cubicle separate. I scan right and left, and arousal rises up and slides through my system. I'm glad I put my thong back on because I'm getting wetter by the minute.

We stop to watch two men having sex. They're in the missionary position, and their eyes are locked on each other. They moan and grunt their pleasure. The man on top issues a warning that he's on the edge, and he grasps the bottom's cock. We stay until they come together with a shout. They seem to be oblivious to the people watching.

"You're not shocked?" Taylor asks in a soft voice.

I think about the question, and I'm pleased with my response. "Not at all. Both of them seemed to be enjoying themselves."

He kisses the top of my head. "Good girl."

I recheck both sides of the aisle. "It's hard to decide what or whom to watch."

He guides me down a few feet to where two naked women are lavishing their attention on one man. He's restrained, his eyes are closed, and his breathing is raspy. The only thing he's wearing is a cock ring. I move closer and observe for a minute since I've never seen one in use.

We continue our tour, stopping and observing straight sex to fetish. I realize my club outfit is not nearly as bold as I suspected. One woman is dressed in only a pair of black stilettos. She's lying on a padded table with one man suckling her breast, a second loudly slurping at her pussy, and a third is sucking on her big toe.

Taylor is standing behind me. His hands slip around my waist. "What do you think about that scene?"

"That wasn't on my list, but it doesn't interest me."

"The idea of three men dedicated to your pleasure doesn't pique your interest just a little?"

I turn my head and look up at him. "That wasn't what I meant. I'd insist they keep my toes out of their mouths."

He buries his head in my neck to muffle his laughter. "So noted."

I lean back into him at the next scene. Feeling him hard as a stone adds to the moisture seeping into my panties as we watch two women taking turns sucking and licking one man's penis. They pass it back and forth like it's an ice cream cone.

Taylor emits a low moan.

"So, two women servicing you isn't objectionable?"

He clears his throat. "Only if you were one of them."

"Good answer."

"Let's move on."

I hear a woman cry out, and I glance up at Taylor. He turns us toward the sound. We see a naked woman bent over a padded table. The man strikes her with a wooden paddle so hard I cringe. She shrieks, and then he drops the wooden paddle. Moving closer, he runs his hands over her bright pink ass.

"Do you want me to fuck you?" His tone is demanding.

"Only if it pleases you, Sir."

"It pleases me to turn this gorgeous ass bright red."

"Then more, please, Sir."

Her Dom is wearing skintight jeans and no skirt. The bulge visible in the front of his pants is prominent. He walks to a black bag sitting on a table and brings out a riding crop.

"Spread your legs wider."

She complies and everyone watching can now see the juices running from her.

He slides the crop between her legs and smacks her pussy with it

"Yes. Thank you, Sir."

He moves it across her butt, upper thighs, and back before spanking her between the legs again. "Do you need to come?"

"Please."

The sound of her softly crying upsets and confuses me.

The Dom turns the crop around and rubs her clit with the handle. "Come now."

Her body jerks and twists and her screams fill the air. When she calms down, he removes the restraints, lifts her in his arms, and walks away.

"Aftercare," Taylor says.

"It hurt my chest to watch. I struggle with understanding how the woman could enjoy that."

"Yet, she didn't use her safe word."

"I'm not judging. I just don't understand."

"I know. You're the most nonjudgmental person I've ever met."

***

We continue our tour, stopping at the next scene. I'd read about the use of hot wax and was about to see it firsthand. A naked man is strapped to a table, and a woman, I'm assuming his Domme, is dripping hot wax on his body. She takes a step sideways and smiles as droplets land on his rigid cock. His loud moans sound more like cries of pain to me, but she doesn't stop, and he doesn't use a safe word. How can he have an erection?

All I can do is stare. "I'm not sure I'll ever be interested in this."

Taylor turns me to face him. Worry clouds his eyes. "I'm not into this kind of pain, either. Do you want me to take you home?"

"What if I don't want to go home yet?"

"No?"

"Not yet." Almost of its own accord, my hand rubs his erection up and down. "We came here to be together, Sir."

Taylor jerks me against his chest, grasps the back of my head, and kisses me. He possesses me with his tongue and mouth. Fire flares to life, licking through my blood. I want him with a passion that consumes every fiber in my being. He releases me, and I'm lost without his touch.

"Let's ask about one of those private rooms."

"Are we allowed since we're guests?"

Taylor grabs my hand. "I don't know, but we'll find out."

We turn around to walk back to the bar, but everyone we pass is going in the other direction.

One of the two men we watched in the first scene pauses. "The demonstration is about to start."

"Kayla and Nick."

"We should watch."

Taylor nods, reading my thoughts. "Let's stay out of sight. I don't know if Kayla will be uncomfortable with me there."

"Good idea."

We aren't sure where to go, so we follow the stragglers to a small stage in a corner. One spotlight hangs over the area, giving the space a slightly foreboding look. Many seats are taken, so Taylor picks up one from the back row and moves it to the end of one aisle. He sits and pats his knee.

"I need to feel you close to me."

"Me too." I wiggle my butt as I make myself comfortable. His erection has gone down a little, but it immediately springs to life with my movements.

"Do you know what happens to a sub who teases her Dom?"

"No. What?" My short skirt has ridden up, baring me except for the tiny thong I wear. The feel of his slacks against my skin feels so good I clench and release my cheeks.

"They get their sweet ass spanked," he whispers. His warm breath against my ear magnifies his warning. "You did check that you're interested in trying everything on the list."

Before I can respond, Nick and Kayla come forward into the light at center stage. All talking stops.

Nick is wearing tight, black leather pants and boots. The muscles in his arms and shoulders ripple with each movement. Kayla is wearing a black robe tied at the front. It's exactly like the one Morgan left for me to wear tonight.

Her hands are clasped behind her back, and her head is lowered. My bawdy, opinionated, feminist friend is showing her submission to her Dom. My heart rate picks up. Doing this of her own free will and knowing she can stop it at any time must be freeing. Maybe the lifestyle is just all about choices.

****

Neither of them speaks or acknowledges the audience. Instead, they keep their gazes locked on each other. Then, a second light comes on, flooding a Saint Andrew's Cross and the restraints waiting for their use. Nick pulls Kayla into a kiss that seems to heat the room and last forever. He lifts his head and says something to her we can't hear. She smiles at him, unties the robe, shrugs her shoulders, and lets it fall to the floor. She's naked except for her collar.

Nick leads her to the cross, where she spreads her legs and lifts her arms. He cuffs her wrists and ankles and then runs his finger around each to make sure they're not too tight. Again, he says something we can't hear, and then he kisses her forehead and walks out of the light into the darkness.

It feels like he makes her wait forever before anything happens. I don't know if it's to build her anticipation or to give her a chance to gather herself.

The sound of the whip's cracks and pops echoes through the darkness. Once. Twice. "Shit." I tense up. I can't see Nick, nor can Kayla, but we know he's there.

Then Nick crosses the floor back to her, casually dragging the cat-o'-nine-tails behind him. With his free hand, he caresses and massages her ass, upper thighs, and back. He steps back a few feet and lifts his arm over his head. With a fluid movement, the whip sails through the air in a figure-eight pattern before just the tips touch her skin. Kayla moans, and he repeats the process.

I hold my breath as, over and over, each lash seems to get harsher, and the red stripes on her body become more prominent.

Taylor's hand slides my thong to the side, and his fingers gently stroke my pussy. I start moving in time with each strike.

Nick drops his arm, allowing the length of the whip to land on the floor next to him. He asks her for a color.

"Green, Sir. I need to come."

"No. You'll come when I say." His arm raises, and the black leather snaps as he teases her with it.

"Yes, Sir."

Kayla's moan draws my attention when she gets louder, and I turn my head, looking to Taylor for answers.

"He's not going to hurt her. Notice the whip hasn't touched her lower back. He could damage that area, so he's being cautious."

A few more loud cracks of the whip and Kayla's ass is bright red, and she's crying out Nick's name. He drops the whip to the floor, releases her, and gathers her in his arms. His lips are on top of her head as he whispers. Then he turns on his heel and carries her from the stage.

"Where's he taking her?"

"To a private room where he'll allow her to come. Then he'll make her comfortable until she's completely recovered."

I turn to face him. Placing my palms on his cheeks, I ask, "Will I be pushing my sub status if I want to try out one of the private rooms before we go home?"

"Not tonight. I think it's a great idea."

I shift in his lap. "I'm sorry for the huge wet spot I left on your slacks."

He laughs that laugh of his, which is spontaneous and sexy as hell. "There are two wet spots. My cock has been leaking since you sat down and shifted with each swing of the whip."

I reluctantly get off his lap and tug down my skirt. Taylor slides a hand under and squeezes the globe of my ass.

"I really like this outfit."

I'm feeling brave, strong, and daring. "Me too, but I'll like it better when you take it off me."

Taylor returns the chair to its designated spot, and we walk up front to the booths.

"Wait here, and I'll see about getting a private room."

"I won't budge."

Taylor stops at the bar and chats with the manager, Danielle, for a minute before following her into a private room. The bartender pours my wine and passes it to a man sitting close to me.

He gets off the stool, turns, and walks toward me. I see it's Slider. His movements scream Dom, but I have trouble thinking of him as anything other than Superman. He eases into the booth next to me and sets the glass of wine in front of me.

"Thank you. I didn't know you were here." I want to ask him where he left his cape.

"Zack and Morgan left for a charity function, and Nick and Kayla are occupied, so I'm manning the helm tonight."

"My two favorite couples."

"Would I be too forward if I mentioned you're stunning tonight?"

His eyes blaze a trail over every inch of my body that's exposed. Thank goodness the table hides the fact my skirt barely covers anything.

"Thanks. I can't imagine you worrying about being forward." He's smoking hot and knows it.

"It kills me that Taylor got to you first."

"Got to me?"

"Wrong choice of words. I wanted to ask you out a long time ago."

"Yet, you didn't."

"Let's just say I've been discouraged by mutual friends from approaching you. Maybe they don't trust me with an innocent like you."

"And now it's too late." It's time to stop being flattered by his boldness.

A grin spreads across his face, and I admit my heart skips a beat.

"Is it?"

I nod simply because my tongue is tied in a knot. Slider is not my type. He's an old-fashioned heartbreaker.

"Taylor is a lucky bastard. He's also a great guy." He nods at someone behind me. I turn my head and see Taylor walking in my direction. Slider stands and offers me his hand. "It was nice seeing you."

I shake his hand and hide my surprise at the tiny spark that travels up my wrist. The two men talk before Slider returns to the bar. Then Taylor takes my hand and helps me stand.

"Are we going to look at the rooms?"

"We are. Danielle has one that's open for the next hour."

Every nerve in my body sends hot streaks racing through my body. I hold his fingers tightly as we turn down a hall toward the back of the building. We walk past the stage into an area that reminds me of a doctor's office.

"If the room is in use, the red light above the door will be on. But if the door is open and a member is interested in joining, they wait until the occupants either invite them in or indicate they should move on."

We walk slowly, checking out the different rooms. Seeing a couple in a doctor/patient role-playing scene is no surprise. Their door is closed, but we can see inside through a window.

"This is like the two-way mirrors you see on police shows. Morgan told me and Kayla about it the day after Zack brought her here for the first time."

"The next room is ours." Taylor steps back. I enter, and he follows, closing the door.

"It looks like an Aladdin's Lamp theme." Purple and turquoise paint covers the walls. Large gold, red, and blue pillows have been tossed randomly across a huge round bed. Lamps with multicolored tassels decorate the corners of the room. One wall looks out of place with whips and paddles of every style and size on display. Across another wall, a long table displays a gold lamp shaped precisely like the one in the fairy tale and a pair of Arabian pointy-toe shoes. There are plenty of drawers and cabinets for storage. The first one I open holds a variety of toys, all packaged in plastic.

"Hermetically sealed." Taylor is standing next to me. I think he's observing my reactions, not what's in the drawers. "Do you know what these are?"

"Vibrators of different sizes?"

"Some vibrate, but they're trainers or butt plugs."

"I read about those." I point to a package of three. "You start with a small one and then graduate to a larger one and then to the largest." I glance at him, and he's grinning down at me. "I have copious amounts of research saved on my laptop. I'm happy to share it with you."

"I've never met a woman as adventurous and open-minded as you are. That's a compliment, not a complaint."

I picked up the package of black rubber plugs and studied them. "One blog said some trainees wear them for days, yet some women don't need any training."

"That depends on the person wearing it and the size of the man's penis."

"It's interesting, but I'm unsure if I'll like it."

Taylor lifts my hair and nuzzles the back of my neck. "There's only one way to find out."

"I guess you're right."

His hand slides under my skirt, and his hand cups my mound. He's done that before, and I love it. It melts my insides, and I feel claimed and protected. He takes my hand and leads me to the bed.

"Undress and get on the bed. I want you on your knees with your head lowered onto the bed."

My legs tremble as I follow instructions. I hear drawers open and close. Taylor moves behind me. His hands massage my butt cheeks and up my lower back.

"The scent of your desire makes me so fucking hard." He slides his fingers forward and back across my pussy before circling my forbidden hole. He spreads my legs wider and then pulls one of my cheeks open, exposing me. "Take deep breaths."

"Oh my God."

"Don't be embarrassed. Every part of your body is beautiful."

I wince as cool liquid drops against my skin. Taylor reaches around me and finds my clit. At the same time, another finger is rubbing circles around my rosebud. I close my eyes and concentrate on deep breathing. More lube is applied, and Taylor's finger slides inside me. He moves in circles, trying to relax my sphincter muscles.

"Talk to me, sweetheart. Words. Color."

Two fingers slide inside my pussy, and a second enters my rear. "Green, Sir." I'm lost to the rapid movements of his fingers. I didn't think I'd enjoy this, but nerve endings I didn't know existed are firing from inside my body. I hear myself moaning while I try to get more of him inside me.

"You are so fucking gorgeous." Then he finds that perfect spot inside me that drives me wild and rubs back and forth.

"That feels so good."

"Still green?"

"Yes, Sir." I gasp for air. "I'm close."

"You are incredible." His body bends over mine, and he kisses me between the shoulder blades. "Come when you're ready. Someday soon, it will be my cock inside your tight asshole, making you cry out."

I press myself back toward him. "I'm... I'm..."

His thumb presses down on my clit, and my entire body shakes and thrashes as explosions of pleasure race through me. I collapse, and Taylor slides his arm under me, holding me steady. His fingers slowly leave my rectum, and he lies down with me at his side. He's murmuring something into my hair, but I can't hear or think. I just am.

I whine when he leaves the bed, but he's back seconds later. Where the wet cloth came from, I have no idea. I know he's gentle as he rolls me to my back, smoothes my hair from my face, and washes me.

"How did I get so lucky that you chose me?" He doesn't wait for an answer. Instead, his mouth covers mine in a claiming kiss. His lips are soft yet firm, and there's no doubt who I belong to.

Then Taylor pulls away, stepping back from the bed. His face lights up with a smile. I recognize the burning lust behind his eyes, and I immediately feel a tingle in my lower belly.

He unbuttons his shirt, turns, and tosses it in the chair next to the bed. The muscles in his back flex with his movements. His arms and chest are works of art, too, but when he removes his slacks, taking his underwear with them, my mouth actually waters. He's thick, long, hard, and mine. He takes his cock in his hand and strokes it slowly.

"May I say something?"

He continues the back-and-forth motion. "Go ahead."

"When you stroke yourself like that, it's the sexiest thing I've ever seen."

"Then I'll do it more often." He climbs onto the bed and moves over me with the grace of a hunting lion. "Knees up. Hold them wide with your hands."

I do as instructed but complain. "Then I can't touch you."

He stops all movement and breathes deeply. "If or when I want you to touch me or talk to me again, I'll let you know."

I do my best to say sorry with my eyes. I think it works because I feel the tip of his dick breach my entrance. He slides inside in slow motion until he's fully sheathed deep inside me, and then he rests his forehead against mine.

"Your pussy is so tight and wet." He pulls back and pauses before setting a rhythm of rapid, mind-blowing thrusts.

I dig my heels into the bed and meet him until our entire world is the sound of skin meeting again and again. I let out a cry of disbelief when he abruptly pulled out.

"Turn over on your side."

I rollover, and he grasps one of my ankles, lifting my leg over his shoulder. He slides inside me, and I discover this angle allows even deeper penetration. I'm impaled on his cock. His movements are hard and fast as he pounds and pounds in me. The warning my body sends isn't a tingle, it's wildfire racing toward a climax. I open my mouth, but no sound comes out.

"Come for me. Come with me."

My pussy clamps down, and my muscle control disappears while I jerk and thrash under him. He doesn't stop, doesn't slow down until he buries himself inside me and pumps his release, filling me with his cum.

Then he gently removes my leg from his shoulder and arranges me on my back. He sinks to the bed next to me, pulling me into his body while we recover. His arm is across my chest, and he cups my breasts in his hands.

"I'm betting we're close to using up the hour we were given."

"Hmm. Time well spent." I feel him smile against my head. "You're probably right."

I remain in place, knowing what's to come. Taylor gets up, wets a few cloths, and returns to clean us up. I get up and dress while he does the same. He's quicker, so he texts Gabriel that we're ready for a ride home.

I do my best to repair my hair and face before giving him my hand and letting him lead me out the door back to the bar. My legs are still shaky, so I cling to his arm.

Gabriel meets us and escorts us to the front door. I glance over my shoulder for one last look at the club and see Slider leaning against the bar. He holds his drink up in salute.

Once outside, Gabriel instructs a driver and orders him to take special care of us. He opens my door, and I slide inside.

"I hope we see you two again soon." He steps back and nods to Taylor as he gets in next to me.

The door barely closes, and the limo moves forward before I remember Slider and Taylor having a quick conversation before we went to the private room. My curiosity gets the best of me. "What were you and Slider whispering about earlier?"

Taylor pushes a button, and the glass shield raises to separate us and the driver.

"You sure you want to know?"

"Well, I am now."

"He offered his services if or when we decide to add a third party to a scene at the club."

My mouth opens, and my lips move, but nothing comes out. Am I upset Slider would be so bold? Or does his offer intrigue me?

Chapter 11

I don't buckle up. Instead, I sit facing Chelsea. "Give me your thoughts on the club."

Her hand rests on my knee. "The club itself is interesting and stimulating. It created a sexual sensory overload for this newcomer."

"That's a perfect description."

"I was surprised at how open people can be about their sexuality, but in every case, the participants were enjoying themselves. Their energy was contagious."

"And the private room?" She glances away, but I don't push her. Her orgasm was huge, but was one night at the club enough to satisfy her curiosity? I hope not. I hope she wants more and with me.

"I want to go back with you as your sub."

If we'd been standing, my knees would have buckled. "You have no idea how proud I am of you. You approach everything with such an open mind and understanding." I release her seat belt. "Come here."

She straddles my lap. "Like this?"

"You are so fucking beautiful. I'm sorry we didn't have more time in the private room. I wasn't finished with you."

"It's kind of private here in the limo." She pulls the thin strip of material covering the top of her breasts down and presents her rose-colored nipples to me.

I spend equal time licking and sucking each one until she's begging for more. Her skirt has already ridden up, and I search out the Velcro bows on her thong and release the sides, baring her pussy. My hand cups her mound. She moans and moves her hips tighter against me.

"Mine." I tighten my grip on her soft skin. "You are mine."

"Yes, Sir."

"Unzip my pants and take out my cock."

She does exactly as I ask and then starts stroking me. "You're still so hard."

"Guide me into your pussy."

Her small, delicate hands line the head of my cock up, and she slides down to the base in one movement.

I pull her face to mine and swallow her loud moan with a kiss. With my hands on her hips, I set a rapid pace, slamming her down hard and then lifting her back up. She starts making those unintelligible sounds that turn me inside out.

"I'm not going to last long." I take her hand and stick two fingers in my mouth, getting them nice and wet, and then press them just past her mound. I place her other hand on her breast. Pleasure yourself while I fuck what's mine."

The sight of her squeezing her nipple and rapidly rubbing her clit almost sets me off. I grip her hips and hold her body still while I ravage her pussy, pounding harder with each thrust. Her mouth opens in a silent scream, and she clamps down on my cock like she's never letting me leave.

I come hard and long. I replace her hand with mine and push her into a second orgasm as my cock pulses inside her.

She collapses forward. We're soaking wet with sweat and completely sated. I hold her, wanting to keep her in my arms, but eventually, I lift her head. "That was impressive."

She moans. "I think we came out of Silken strung a little tight."

I laugh. "Ya think? We should face our next challenge soon."

"And that is?"

"Reaching the bin where the used wipes are kept from this side of the limo."

Chelsea snickers. "Watching you scoot anywhere has never entered my mind. But you're right. We need to clean up our mess on this limo seat, or the driver will know what we've been doing."

I pull her in for a kiss before edging my way far enough that I can reach the wipes. "You know he knows what's been happening back here?"

"Of course he is, but we don't have to acknowledge it."

"Point taken." We both take a wipe, and we're good to go in seconds.

The limo slows to a crawl. "You're staying, aren't you?"

"Try to chase me away."

"Good." She lifts her thong up and dangles it on the tip of her finger. "Too late to put this back on."

I take it from her, bring it to my face, and breathe in before pushing it into my pocket.

"Gross." Her face scrunches up in disgust.

"There's nothing gross about your scent. Nothing. Got it?"

She lowers her head slightly, but not before I see her smile. "Yes, Sir."

The limo stops, and a few seconds later, our door opens. I exit, and Chelsea slides out, wrapping her cape around her shoulders. I thank the new driver and wrap my arm around her as we walk inside. I feel a shiver race across her body.

She pushes the elevator call button. Her hand comes up to cover her mouth as a yawn escapes. The general excitement of the night has her coming down from her high. I'll wrap her in my arms and ensure she sleeps well tonight.

****

I open my eyes and learn two things. It's daylight, and Chelsea's long hair is tickling my armpit. I stay very still, content to watch her sleep. She's probably exhausted after last night. I woke her twice for midnight sex, but the third time was the best. She took the initiative. I woke with my cock in her mouth.

She rolls onto her other side, and I follow her, spooning our bodies. I slide my hand over her hip, then between her legs, and cup her soft, warm mound in my hand. "Mine," I whisper.

"Yours."

I lift my head to see if I disturbed her sleep, but her eyes are closed, and her breathing is even. That she was talking in her sleep makes her words all the more powerful. My body relaxes, and I decide a few more hours of rest won't hurt either of us.

****

The aroma of bacon pulls me awake. I opened my eyes to find a beautiful woman wearing my T-shirt from last night. She's holding a slice of the breakfast delicacy under my nose. I groan my appreciation.

Chelsea puckers her lips into a pout. "Did somebody wear you out last night, or do you always sleep until ten o'clock on Sunday morning?"

I grab her and pull her on top of me. "Who wore whom out?"

She grins down at me. "Yes, but I'm younger than you."

"Only by a couple of years." I try to snag a bite of the bacon dangling from her fingers, but she pulls it out of my reach. "You're just asking to get that tiny little ass of yours spanked."

She leans up onto her elbows. "You are not spanking me whether my ass is tiny or not."

"Excuse me, sassy girl?" My brows lift to appear stern. "And why won't I?"

"Because your eggs, bacon, and cinnamon rolls will get cold."

"Homemade or out of a can?"

"You'll have to come downstairs and see for yourself." She leans down and kisses me. It's soft and sweet, with just a hint of tongue.

I can't count the ways she pleases me.

I draw in a full breath and release it with a fake sigh. "I guess your punishment can wait until later."

"You are too kind, Sir."

I hear a ding, and she leaps off me.

"That's the timer. You have five minutes."

She thunders down the stairs, sounding more like an elephant than the dainty woman who can't weigh much more than a hundred and ten pounds. I rush through the bathroom, slide on my slacks from last night, and join her in the kitchen.

Barefoot, with her hair in a messy knot on top of her head, the sleeves from my shirt rolled up, and the bottom almost reached her knees. "You are so beautiful."

"Thank you." She points to the fridge. "Milk or juice? Your choice."

"Coffee?"

"The carafe is on the table next to the fruit plate."

She stacks plates of food on a kitchen towel draped over her arm and walks to the table. Personally, I can barely manage two, but she's got it mastered. I grab a couple of mugs, bring an unopened bottle of orange juice from the fridge, and carry them to the dining area.

I pull out her chair and kiss her neck when she sits. "Thank you for fixing breakfast. I'm starving."

"I like to cook for hungry people."

She scoops two rolls from a pan and places them in the center of my plate. I fill the outer ring with eggs and bacon. Then I take a big bite of the roll and moan my appreciation. "These are amazing. My mother used to make them, but it took hours. How did you manage?"

"I bought a can of pizza dough at the grocery store, flattened it into a rectangle, and the rest was just adding butter, cinnamon, and sugar."

"You make it sound so easy. They are delicious." I spot a bit of icing clinging to her bottom lip, so I lick it off with my tongue. "That tasted even better."

She stabs a chunk of pineapple and feeds it to me. "Did you know the flavor of what you eat can be reflected in the taste of your cum?"

I try to swallow and laugh at the same time. It results in me choking and coughing for a few seconds. "Well, that was random," I say after catching my breath. "Are you lodging a complaint?"

Chelsea forks a chunk of pineapple and pops it into her mouth. I wait while she chews.

"No." She rolls her eyes. "I read it in several blogs and decided to try it out."

"Exactly how much does one have to eat before it makes a difference?"

"I don't recall. But a person should eat fruit every day anyway."

We finish our breakfast in silence, with me paying particular attention to the pineapple. I'm up for anything that gets her lips wrapped around my cock.

"That was the best meal I've had in a long time. How did you know that cinnamon rolls are my favorite?"

"I didn't. Lucky guess."

"You're thinking this would get you out of being punished?" I can't quite get a read on her. She has almost convinced me she's interested in experiencing a spanking.

"Maybe." She starts stacking plates. "We're not handwashing this time."

"Good idea."

Together, we get the table cleared and the dishes loaded. She pushes the button on the dishwasher, and the soft hum of the machine ends our breakfast.

Chelsea pauses as we leave the kitchen. "Do you still want to talk about last night? If so, I'm ready when you are."

I pull her into my arms and bury my face in her soft neck. "Would you like to go somewhere, maybe to the park, or we can crash on the couch?"

"The couch."

I sit at the end so she can be close or distance herself. She sits in the middle, turning sideways with her feet tucked under her butt.

"Will you tell me how you feel or think after the trip to Silken?"

She levels her gaze on me. "I answered that last night."

"That was then. Sometimes, things look different in the daylight."

"Not to me. If you're there, so am I."

I nod. "I'll fill out the paperwork tomorrow."

She puts her hand on my knee. "But what about when we're not at the club?"

"Scenes in the bedroom are between Dom and sub. Occasionally, would I be thrilled to walk through the door and find you in the submissive position? Hell, yes."

"What about punishments?"

"Punishments come in many forms. Some Doms use humiliation, which is something I'm not into. Making you stand naked facing a corner of the room isn't how I want to see you. Nor will I pour dry, uncooked rice on the floor and make you kneel on it for hours."

She frowns.

"I'm not beyond edging, but not as a discipline. It can result in a powerful orgasm."

"And spanking?"

"Of course. If a sub has to be corrected for the same thing over and over, a Dom might paddle her butt. But spankings can also heighten your desire. If you're into a little pain, it can morph into pleasure."

"Are you really going to spank me today?"

"You did insinuate I'm old."

She shrugs her shoulders. "That I did."

God, I love how playful she can be. "Then you'd better stretch out across my thighs and get it over with. Ten spanks should do it."

She ducks her head. Then she pulls her legs out from under her and crawls over me. My cock is getting harder by the second, and by the time she's in position, I'm stone. I pull the shirt she's wearing up over her ass and fuck me if she's not bare.

"You've been running around here without panties ever since I got up?" I grasp one cheek and squeeze. "You would've been my breakfast if I'd known."

"I wanted you to eat it while it was hot."

It took a second before she realized what she said. We laugh, and I take the opportunity to adjust her body so I can slide my hand under her. "You are soaking, love. Let's see if I can warm you up even more."

The first swat is easy, and she wiggles her ass on my lap. She asked me the other day if that was all I had, and I won't set myself up for that question again. The next slap is more brutal.

"Color?"

"Green, Sir."

By the time we get to ten smacks, her ass is a beautiful pink. I pull her into my arms and discover she's smiling, but tears are running down her cheeks. We need to discuss this. I rock her in my arms. "It's over. Will you tell me why you're crying?"

"I don't know."

"But we need to know."

She lies back in my arms so she can see me. "Something inside me relaxed, and I accepted you were in charge. I was safe. I had no decisions to make and nothing to worry about. A sense of relief washed over me. The promotion I didn't get, or my new boss, whoever it is, didn't feel so important."

I don't try to explain or analyze her emotions. Instead, I hold her tighter and let her work through what's happening inside her head. If there's more, she'll tell me when she's ready. Then her eyes close, and she dozes in my arms.

Her cell buzzes, and I just let it vibrate. No way am I waking her. I'm not sure how long I hold her before I lean my head back and doze off myself. The soft touch of something walking through my chest hair has me opening my eyes.

"Hello." Chelsea's fingers slide up to my chin. "Isn't your arm asleep by now?"

"Doesn't matter. Stay where you are. I'm not complaining."

"I have to go to the bathroom. If I don't, your only pair of pants here will be in jeopardy."

I could get used to waking up to her sense of humor. "Then I suggest you get moving."

She places her lips at the corner of my mouth in the softest, sweetest kiss I've ever had and then stands. "Yes, Sir."

"Your phone rang once."

"Be right back." She grabs her cell and jogs to the bathroom. Minutes later, she's back in the living room with a toothbrush in her mouth. "Morgan wanted to know how last night went."

"And?"

"I told her it was stupendous." Chelsea wipes toothpaste from the corner of her mouth, holds up one finger, and darts out of sight.

"That's an awfully big word coming from such a petite woman." I will draw a reaction, so I stand and start counting it down. One. Two. Three. And she's back with her hands on her hips.

"I may buy from the petite racks, but I'll have you know that under these clothes is a..."

I can't hold back my laugh, and she punches me in the chest. "A tiger. A tiger with a big heart. You, my darling, are perfect."

"The word *such* is what got you in trouble."

I slide my hands under her arms and lift her. Her legs lock around my waist, and her hands around my neck. "You need to send me home. It's not masculine to admit it, but I have scullery maid duties, as you call them. Sadly, nobody washes, dries, and folds my underwear."

Chelsea starts rocking her hips from side to side. "You're stranded."

"I am?"

"Your car isn't here."

"And you're not driving me home."

"I'm not?"

"No. You have things to do, too."

"That's no fun."

By now, my shirt has worked its way up, and she's rubbing her pussy against my zipper. "I was pretty rough on you a couple of times last night. You're not too sore?"

Her eyes light up with that sparkle she has when she's about to get her way. "No, Sir."

I turn around and push her against the wall. "Good, because I really need to be inside you." I lift her higher with one hand and finally get my dick out of my pants. I rub the head back-and-forth, getting us both ready.

"Put me inside you."

She moans a soft, erotic sound and maneuvers herself exactly where she needs to be. The second I feel my head at her entrance, I release the hand that was holding her higher and slam inside her. She cries out as every inch of me fills her.

Then she buries her face in my neck and bites me. "So good. More. Please."

Somewhere along the way, we turn into animals. Licking, biting, scratching, and driving each other to the point where nothing else exists but the two of us.

"Oh God. Taylor."

"Come with me." I change the angle of my body just enough to hit her G-spot with every thrust. Her head falls back, and she cries out my name again. I jump into the abyss with her.

Then I stumble back to the couch and sit where we were minutes ago. Neither of us speaks until our breathing slows. "I'm making a new rule. You're not allowed to wear panties in my presence."

"It will simplify things." She chuckles. "Taylor?"

"Hmm?"

"Your shirt looks like you slept in it for a week."

I look down at the disheveled woman still wearing the wrinkled shirt I wore last night. "It will give the Uber driver something to think about."

Chapter 12

Chelsea

It's a typical Monday at work, and my boss keeps me busy, clearing all projects off his calendar. Then he buzzed me, and I grabbed my iPad and headed to his desk.

"You won't need that." He shakes his head and waves me to the chair across from him.

I sit on the edge, not just a little spooked at the seriousness of his drawn eyebrows and thinned lips. "Has something happened?"

"As with most companies, when a ranking member of management who has access to private and proprietary material retires or quits, they are dismissed and told to leave. Security should be getting off the elevator soon."

"Son of a bitch."

He smiles, probably shocked at my language. "Exactly. In truth, I'm surprised it didn't happen the day I announced my retirement. If I cannot gather my personal things, will you box up my family pictures, books, and such? You'll have to leave them downstairs in the security office so I can pick them up."

"Of course I will." I'm battling tears of disappointment, but mainly, anger is leaking from my eyes. "How dare they treat you this way after all the hours, days, and years you've given this company?"

"Director Ware will be the interim VP, and he'll likely get the promotion."

"He's a jerk."

"Which is why I wanted to tell you myself."

He stands, and I do the same.

"I know this is not professional, but..." I don't finish my sentence. Instead, I walk around behind his desk and hug him. "I will never have another boss I respect as much as you."

"Thank you."

I turn and leave the office, pausing to snarl and comment to the guard arriving at the door.

When they're ready to leave, I walk him to the elevator, noticing he's carrying a box with his personal belongings. A quick wave and then the doors close. I stand in the hallway for a minute, go to the lady's room, clean up my face, and then return to my desk. The office behind me is dark. I picked up my phone to text the president's assistant that I was leaving early and saw that my mom had called twice. She texts but never calls me at work. I sit and return her call, worried.

"I don't have but a second. Your dad had a slight stroke earlier this week, and we're coming home."

My brain is about to explode. "Define 'slight.'"

"Oh, hell." My dad's gruff voice drowns out Mom's. "Give me the damn phone before you scare her to death."

"Hi, pumpkin."

"Truth, Dad."

"We're on an airplane in Frankfurt. We take off in a few minutes. I had a mini-stroke that lasted a few minutes. I spent a couple of nights in a German hospital, where I almost starved. I'm taking two different drugs and have to see my doctor as soon as we get home."

"Rest if you can. That's a long flight."

"And I plan on sleeping through most of it. The tour company upgraded us to first class. We're flying in style."

I hear a flight attendant's voice in the background. "Okay. What's your flight number?"

"Hell, if I know. Why?"

"Ask Mom. Hurry."

"It's 1483."

"I'll be in Kauai before you arrive, so I'll pick you up at the airport."

"You'll do no such thing."

"Love you, Dad." I end the call, no doubt leaving him grumbling. I notified human resources I had a family emergency and requested a two-week vacation. I straighten my desk, grab my handbag, and hurry to the elevator.

After the accident, my dad put on a lot of weight, and his doctor has cautioned him many times about his high blood pressure. I can only hope it truly was a slight stroke. My nerves have my stomach in knots. I stop at a red light and dial Morgan. I explained what was going on and asked her to let Kayla know.

"Take a deep breath," Morgan instructs. "You won't be any help to anyone if you kill yourself in traffic."

"I'm okay. Dad sounded as if it was nothing, but that's his way. Mom's tone of voice makes me think it's more serious than he wants me to know. And I have vacation hours to burn. After I get there and see how serious his situation is, I'll decide if I want to stay the full two weeks or return early. "

"Have you called Taylor?"

"I'll do that after I get to my apartment."

"Be safe. And stay in touch!"

"I will."

"Love you!" she calls out.

As my mom always says, I do my best not to borrow trouble. When I reach my apartment building and park my car, I mentally try to decide what to pack for the trip while I walk inside, and by the time I enter my apartment, I'm organized.

I unlock my door and step inside before pulling my cell from my purse and calling Taylor.

"Are you packed?"

"Not yet. I waited until I got home to call you to talk while I put clothes in my suitcase. I shouldn't have told Morgan first."

"Wait. Please don't think I'm upset you didn't call me first. This is about you, your family, and what you need. That's all I care about."

"Thank you. All I have to do is pack and buy a ticket to Kauai." My chest squeezes. "Oh my God. In my panic, I failed to put first things first. I have to hang up and call the airlines. What if there's not a flight out today?"

I've never felt so stupid.

"Chelsea, baby! Take a deep breath. You don't need to call the airlines. The company jet will be ready when you are."

"What?

"Zack has the jet pilot drawing up the flight plan right now. I'll be at your apartment in five minutes. Go start packing."

I sigh of relief, knowing I'll see him for a few minutes before I leave. My chest tightened when I realized he'd left work early to be with me for a few minutes. What a time to discover I'm in love with him.

I open my mouth to argue but see he's ended the call. I immediately call Morgan.

"Don't start," she says instead of hello. "What's the point of having a billionaire for a husband if I can't help a friend?"

"That's not why you married him. And it's damn sure not why we're friends."

"Chels. Stop. It's okay to let somebody help you. Think of it this way. The plane is parked in the hangar doing nothing, and neither is the pilot."

I take a deep breath, knowing my outburst was rude. "I'm sorry for biting your head off. I know you're just being kind, and I love you for it."

"I get it. Go take care of your family and keep in touch."

"I will. Tell Zack I appreciate him so much, and I'll never be able to repay his kindness."

"Oh, honey. Don't worry about it. Go!"

I take off my work clothes while climbing the stairs to my bedroom. I drop them in the closet on the floor and kick off my heels. Then I slip on a pair of leggings, an extra-long shirt, and tennis shoes for the long flight.

My suitcase is big enough for a couple of weeks' worth of clothing. I drag it out and toss it on my bed. I grab my carry-on and fill it with makeup, one change of clothes, and a pair of sandals in case my luggage is lost. My laptop, e-reader, iPad, and three different types of chargers go on top. I pull hangers of clothes from the closet and start packing everyday wear.

"I'm not sure I want to see a bikini in that suitcase, but you should take one."

I'm in his arms before he finishes his sentence. I feel his strength as he gathers me tightly. Finally, tears seep from my eyes, and I try to blink them away.

"I'm sorry. I'm sure your dad will be okay. He'll have you to keep him in line."

Taylor takes a step back and thumbs my cheeks dry.

"I hope I'm overreacting."

"What did your mom say?" Taylor turns me around toward my suitcase. "Keep packing while you talk."

A small smile creeps up on me at his commanding tone. "I'm almost done. I didn't get to talk to Mom much because Dad took over. She'd tried to reach me earlier, but I was with my boss helping clear his desk and didn't hear my cell ring. They were getting ready for takeoff when I reached her. She said he'd had a mini-stroke. My dad, of course, insists it was minor." I put the last piece of clothing in my bag, close it, and snap the locks. "There was something in my mom's tone of voice, though. I'm worried they're not telling me everything."

Taylor lifts my suitcase as if it weighs nothing and slips the strap of my carry-on bag over his shoulder. "You take care of my girl. Come back to me."

"I will." I lead him from my apartment to the elevator and outside. My heart aches knowing how far away I'll be, but I also know I must be with my parents. "I'll miss you."

"Say that again when I get you to the airport."

"You're driving me?"

"Of course."

"You're too good to me."

"I'll think of ways you can repay me after you get home."

"Deal." There's an ache deep in my chest, and I almost blurt out how much I care about him, but I don't. Instead, I decide it's just a combination of fear for my dad and sadness I won't have Taylor with me.

He opens my door for me and then places my luggage in the trunk of his car. After he gets in and we're driving away from my complex, he asks me more about my family, and in the middle of his sentence, I gasp. "I don't know if Mom called my sister or not. She'll be furious if nobody tells her."

"Do you think you should check on her?"

I drag my fingers through my hair, unseating the messy bun I wear for work. I do my best to fix it and then give up. "My folks wouldn't want her leaving school, so I'm going to wait until I see firsthand what the situation is at home."

He takes his cell from the console and hands it to me. "If it's okay, I'd like the name and address of the bed and breakfast, as well as a phone number."

I reach across the car and stroke his cheek with my knuckles. "You can ask and get anything you want from me."

"I'll hold you to that."

I enter the information into his cell and place it back in his console. "I only have one number for you."

"Open my briefcase. It's on the back seat."

"Okay?"

"Take out the small card case and open it."

I hold the silver case with his initials engraved on the top. I flip open the lid and take out his business card—cream colored with dark-brown, embossed lettering. The paper is thick and smooth.

"It's beautiful. Looks expensive."

"The case and cards were on my desk the first day I started. That's my office number. Call Zack if you have to."

Taylor rests his open hand on the console, and I wind my fingers through his. His strength makes me stronger. "God, I'm going to miss you."

Before I can respond, he's turning onto the street, leading to a row of small planes. "Have you ever flown on a private jet?"

"No. But I'm guessing it's going to be plush as hell inside. I'm sure they'll take good care of you."

"Morgan said it was like flying on a magic carpet." My mind jumps to the Arabian Nights room at Silken. "Oh my God, do you think she and Zack have—"

Taylor's laugh ends my thought. "I'd say it's quite possible."

I wave my hand in front of my face. "I'm erasing that image from my mind."

Taylor parks in front of a small office building. Then he exits the car and removes my luggage from his trunk. He walks to my door and opens it. Dropping into a squat, he reaches across me and unhooks my seatbelt. "You go take care of your family. As much as I'll miss you, it's the right thing to do."

I cup his face to kiss him and hear the door to the building open and close. A woman wearing dark slacks and a crisp white blouse walks toward us. Her hair is dark and pulled back in the same way I wear mine. I step out of the car and walk to meet her.

She extends her hand. "Ms. Coffman?"

"Yes." I grasp her palm, appreciating the good grip she has.

"We're ready for you to board. Is this all the luggage you're taking?"

"Yes."

"I'm Mara Waybourn. I'm your captain for the flight."

"I'm ready."

Captain Waybourn takes both my suitcase and overnight bag from Taylor. Then she turns and walks to the plane.

Taylor's arm slides around my waist. "Talk soon."

I lift onto my tiptoes, pull his face to mine, and kiss him with everything I have. "Talk soon."

"Go."

I walk away, fighting the urge to turn and take one extra look at him. Then I shove away the gnawing pain in my gut at leaving him behind.

Chapter 13

Taylor

I reread the text Chelsea sent last week after she'd landed at Princeville Airport on Kauai. She was surprised to find a rental car waiting for her. I can see her cruising down the Kuhio Highway, top-down, in the red convertible, sunglasses shading her gorgeous eyes. And a frown wrinkling her forehead.

She'd arrived hours before her parents' plane landed, so she'd driven to their bed and breakfast in Kapa'a to settle in before making the trip back to Lihue Airport to collect them. Seeing her dad walk off the airplane with no more help than a walker put her mind at ease.

She said she would stay long enough to help her mother and be sure her dad followed the doctor's orders. I understand, but it doesn't make me miss her any less.

I've reminded Chelsea several times over text that she belongs to me and there will be consequences if she doesn't take good care of herself.

I received a blushing smiley face and her promise.

Zack strolls into my office and sits across from me. "I should have sent you with her."

"I just started this job."

"Money or this position isn't why you don't go to her. If her father's health is serious, she'll welcome you being there." Zack steeples his hands and looks at the ceiling for a minute. "But I guess that depends on how you feel about her."

"It's not that, not at all. I'm thrilled you and Morgan stepped up and helped Chelsea. No doubt the red convertible waiting on her at the airport was Morgan's doing, and it cheered her up. I don't mean to sound ungrateful. I appreciate the hell out of what you've done for me already."

"You're going to earn everything you get." Zack smiles as he rises from the chair. "Someday, and I hope it's not too far down the road, I'm retiring. Then, I'm going to spend my time keeping my wife happy. Silken, and maybe Gallants, will be under our watchful eyes."

"Gallants? What about Slider?"

"Slider's talking about opening a second adult club and naming it Satin."

"I'm not surprised."

"As far as your responsibilities, you'll take over here. Understand that being out of the office for a week or two will not change things here."

Then he walks out of my office and disappears down the hall.

My desk phone buzzes, telling me Mrs. Hayden is on the line. She's the office manager/expert on every job function in this place. She and Zack have the best working relationship I've ever seen. He's positive she could manage the business without any trouble. She might have been his first choice, but she's in her sixties and flatly refused to take on the responsibility.

This brokerage firm is not a large company by design. Over the years, Zack has built up close relationships with clients and has intentionally kept his business small enough so that each one gets our full attention.

I press the button on the phone. "Yes, ma'am?"

"Your ten o'clock is here." Her voice is a whisper. "Do you need a minute before I escort Ms. Oakland to your office?"

"That bad?"

"Yes, Mr. Horne." Mrs. Hayden's voice could freeze even the warmest coffee.

"Bring her in."

I put my cell on silent, drop it in a desk drawer, and glance at my laptop screen, where I've been reading her file. According to Mrs. Hayden, this client usually does business over the phone, and I'm sure this face-to-face meeting is all about me being new.

I stand as Mrs. Hayden introduces me to an attractive brunette. She looks to be in her early forties, but it's hard to tell. Her body is in great shape, and she's dressed to prove it. Judging by her well-maintained appearance and expensive clothes, I wondered if she knew the business meeting with me or if she expected to see Zack.

Something about her feels familiar.

"It's a pleasure to meet you, Ms. Oakland." I wave to a chair at my conference table in the corner. It's positioned next to a large window, letting the light and warmth of the day inside. "Please be seated. Would you like something to drink? Water? Coffee?"

She levels her gaze on Mrs. Hayden. "If Zack Pierce plans to shove me off on a newbie, the least he can do is provide some of his expensive whiskey."

"Right away," Mrs. Hayden says, turning and looking at me with a question.

"None for me. Thanks."

I move my laptop to the table in front of the chair I'll occupy, but I don't initiate a conversation until Mrs. Hayden delivers the whiskey. She nods and then leaves.

I take my seat and lean back. "I sincerely hope you don't feel shoved off because that's not what happened. I'm confident I can manage your portfolio successfully."

Ms. Oakland sips her drink and stares at me over the rim of the glass. "How old are you?"

For the next few minutes, we play twenty questions, with her asking about me and my personal life and me steering her toward a conversation about her portfolio.

"Getting back to your reason for being here today. Your investments are performing extremely well. Do you have any concerns?"

"I hope you were briefed on the charities I support. I want it understood those donations are private. Only a few people are privileged enough to know. A breach of trust will not only result in you losing my business, but you'll also hear from my attorney."

"I assure you, we take your trust in us very seriously." I ease my chair back. "Your investments are fairly conservative for such a young woman. Are you opposed to considering anything a little risky with the potential for rapid growth?"

She knocks back the last of her whiskey and stands. "Zack used to escort me to an occasional fundraiser until he married." Her gaze rakes over me. "Are you available?"

I also stand, wondering what I should say to that. "If something comes up, contact Mrs. Hayden. She'll always know my schedule." I walk to my desk and hand her a folder ready for her this morning. "If you're interested in growth, I've located a new tech company we should discuss. They're new, fresh, and their finances are great."

She looks at me for a few seconds, and I decide I've blown it with her, but she won't respond.

"I'll think about it." She drops the folder on my desk. "Email me with your research."

Without another word, she walks out of my office.

"You didn't think I was going to let you have my easy clients, did you?" I look up to see Zack leaning against the doorframe. "I wanted you to meet one of our most difficult accounts. She requested the information you offered her but was pissed when I invited her to meet her new financial manager. She'll always push back and try to bully you, but that's just a façade. I think she's lonely and one of the many diverse personalities you'll have to deal with."

"She looked familiar. Who is she, really?"

Zack chuckles as he crosses my office and sits in the same chair he'd used a few minutes ago. "She and her husband were among Silken's first members. He was much older than her, and he died shortly after they joined. She was there the night you and Chelsea were."

"You two were more than friends?"

"No. Ms. Oakland likes to play. Sometimes, she brings a guest. Before Morgan, she occasionally requested Slider or me. Those scenes happened with the understanding that nothing was serious or permanent."

"But you're married, and she's moved on?"

"She moved on before then." Zack grins. "She had eyes for Gabriel for a long time, but he's not interested in the lifestyle."

"He's quite the enigma."

"That's true. I know Gabriel's wife died many years ago. But he doesn't talk about it with anyone." Zack stands. "Have you heard from Chels today?"

"I got a text from her this morning."

"Call her." Zack stands and starts to walk out of the room. Then he stops at the door. "Take the fucking plane and spend a long weekend with her. Better yet, you go with the plane to get her when she's ready to return."

He shuts the door without waiting for any discussion.

I take my cell out of the desk drawer and check my messages. I've missed a text.

I love it here. I wish you could see what I see.

Pictures that look as if they were taken from magazines follow her text. Shots of tall, emerald mountains, sandy beaches, waves crashing onto the sand, and flowers of every color make me miss her even more.

I just saw the pictures. Where's one of you?

I take awful selfies. I was going to call but decided against it while you're at work.

I don't hesitate and decide to FaceTime her. She has been gone for over a week, and it feels much longer. If it wasn't for phone sex, I might have already taken Zack up on his offer. We've survived by watching each other pleasure ourselves. Realizing how much I miss her voice and physical presence has been a revelation.

Her smiling face fills the screen on my cell.

"Hello, gorgeous." Damn, she's glowing. "Looks like you've been getting some sun."

"I've been working in the garden. I'm glad you called. I miss talking to you."

"Me too. How's your dad?"

"Grouchy, but doing great."

"Sounds like he's getting stronger."

"The scare was enough for him to start listening to his doctor. He's working with his physical therapist for his back and has started to walk with a cane. He loves gardening and hopes to take over soon."

"I'm glad. I know your mom must feel better, too."

"Oh, yeah. She's thrilled."

"Does that mean you're coming home soon?"

"This coming Sunday." She tilts her head and stares into the phone. "Morgan called this morning and checked with Zack immediately after hanging up. The jet will bring me home."

"Halle-fucking-lujah."

"Is it bad that I don't like being away from you?"

I want to reach through the phone and drag her into my arms. "Want to know something?"

"Yes, please."

"I miss you more."

She holds the phone close to her face. "You sure you don't just miss my pussy?" she whispers.

I bark out a laugh, and thank God Zack closed the door on his way out. My cock instantly starts swelling. "Yes, I'm sure, but just hearing you say the word *pussy* makes me hard."

"Show me." She's laughing and trying to talk at the same time.

"Now you're getting bossy, you little minx. You'll see it when you get home."

"I can't wait."

"Are you wearing your plug?"

Her cheeks flush, and her eyes sparkle. "Yes, Sir."

"I'm so proud of you for following my instructions."

She'd ordered the set of three after she'd arrived.

"May I remove it?"

"Tonight. Tomorrow morning, move to the next size."

"Chelsea?" I hear a voice in the background.

"In the garden, Mom."

"Go. I'll call you tonight around bedtime."

"K." She blows me a kiss, and then the screen goes dark, and I'm left sitting with a raging hard-on.

That she would buy the plugs is impressive.

That she's lubed and inserted the first two sizes herself blows me away.

That the next one is the largest, and she's done it for me.

I push away from my desk and walk to Zack's office. "Question."

"Fire away."

"Remember that long weekend you suggested I take?"

Chapter 14

Chelsea

I wake to bright sunlight and smile. I can't wait to be home and wake up next to Taylor. I love my parents and Kauai, but I miss my life, friends, and job. But most important of all, I miss my man.

I try to roll over and stretch, but a lump is pressing into my back. Mom's dog must have snuck into my room last night. I push at him with my butt. "Charlie, how did you get in here?"

"Who's Charlie?"

"Taylor!" I squeal. My heart runs wild, and I kick at the covers, freeing myself from the bedsheet. I turn and look into his handsome face. My hands cup his cheeks while my eyes feast on his face, and I place little kisses all over him. "You're here. You're *really* here."

"Instead of Charlie?"

"He's the resident dog."

"I met him downstairs." Taylor pulls me against him, and his mouth crashes down on mine. His lips are soft and demanding and so welcome. I open for him, and our tongues probe as if we haven't been together in months. Then he eases back, his gaze searching my face as if to imprint my image in his mind.

"I can't believe you're in my bed!"

"I won't be here long. Your mom and dad are expecting us downstairs for breakfast."

I snuggle even closer, wishing I could hold him against me forever. I slide my hand between us and grasp his hard-on. "I can't believe my dad let you come up here."

Taylor covers my hand with his, squeezes, and then moves away. "He didn't. Your mom vouched for me."

"Then I guess I'd better get dressed." Reluctantly, I sit up and swing my feet to the floor.

He slides off the bed, walks around to where I'm standing, and cups me between my legs. "Mine."

Tears fill my eyes, and I try to blink them away, but he lifts my chin.

"Talk to me."

"That's such a simple gesture, but it's one of my favorite things that you do. Sometimes, in your sleep, you just hold me. I hadn't realized how much I missed it."

His face softens as he lowers his forehead to mine. "Then I'll never stop doing it." He steps back. "Now get dressed. Your folks don't expect me to stay here while you dress."

"Probably not."

"Throw those plugs away."

"Yay!" I cheer.

"The next thing that will go inside your sweet ass is me."

I watch as his long legs cross the floor to my door. His broad shoulders look like he could carry the world's weight.

He thinks he's left me speechless. "Taylor?"

He turns his head. "Hmm?"

"I'm happy not to have that thing in me for hours." I try to contain my excitement and hurry into my bathroom, where I spend a few minutes longer on my appearance than I have the past week and a half.

I pause and look in the mirror. To say I'm happy Taylor surprised me is an understatement. I slip on a pair of sandals to go with a pair of shorts and a cotton pullover and then follow the aroma of Mom's cooking down the stairs to the kitchen. The staff in the house has already fed the guests and even prepared picnic lunches for a few families up at the main building.

My mom and dad live in the small house behind the bed and breakfast. I open the front door to the sound of Taylor's laughter and know Dad's telling him about all my childhood screwups.

"There's one of my favorite subjects," Dad says as he extends one arm, and I bend down and get a hug.

"Did you hit a fourth-grade boy and wind up in the principal's office?" Taylor asks between chuckles.

"Taylor, I wouldn't lie to you. She had a good right hook back then."

"Well, he never tried to look down my blouse again."

I keep walking, leaving my two men to themselves, and go to check in with my mom.

She is in her element in the kitchen. When she sees me, she turns and points to the cabinet. "Morning, darling. Set the table for me, would you?. These rolls are ready to come out of the oven."

"You're supposed to spoil me, not Taylor." I dodge the dish towel as she intentionally misses me with it. Then, I load the plates, silverware, and napkins before going to the dining room. I put everything in its place and returned to assist her. "What next?"

She puts the pan of rolls on a trivet and turns to me. "He's not only handsome, but he seems to care about you. I like him a lot."

"Me too." I carry the platters of eggs, bacon, and hash browns to the table.

Mom's right behind me with a carafe of juice and a pot of coffee. "Is it serious?"

"Mom," I whine. "I can't answer that."

"You two would make beautiful babies."

"Mom," I repeat, this time without the whine.

She shrugs. "Just saying." Wiping her hands on her apron, she walks into the living room. "You boys, come eat breakfast before it gets cold."

****

The past three days have flown by, passing entirely too fast for me. There is so much to see and do on this island, and I'm disappointed I can't show all of it to Taylor, but we'll take some good memories back to Chicago.

The first day he arrived, I took him to a local store where he bought swim trunks, sandals, and aviator sunglasses. I can't wait to tell Morgan and Kayla about walking down the beach next to him. Women were turning their heads to get a second look at him, and I smiled, knowing he belonged to me. If he had noticed the looks he had gotten, he wouldn't have acted like it.

We've managed to have sex a few times, but since Mom installed him in the room next to their bedroom, it hasn't been easy. We've been discreet and have only had one close call. The bed and breakfast flower garden is large and laid out in a maze so guests can wander through the beauty and have fun. The garden shed is situated at the very back of the area. Behind it, an old bench is there to be sanded and repainted. It seems long forgotten and offers a quiet place to have private time.

The caretaker on staff was working in the front of the main building when I led Taylor to my newly found hiding place. Who expected Dad to show up dragging a flatbed wagon with a load of fertilizer stacked on it? He'd tried to pull a fast one on Mom and unload it into the shed by himself.

Taylor, who stayed utterly calm when the shed door slammed open, left me half-dressed and sitting on a bench so he could help Dad. I managed to escape to the house while Taylor helped him unload the cart.

I love him more every day.

"Need some help?" Mom asks from the doorway.

"I'm packed. And don't be too nice to me. You know we'll both start crying."

She comes closer and wraps her arms around me. "My tears will be different this time. I'm so happy for you and Taylor."

"It's obvious you like him a lot."

"That young man is in love with you. Your happiness takes precedence over everything else. Has he told you yet?"

"No. I'm not sure you're right about that."

"I'm one hundred percent right about him. He might not know it yet, but I do." Then she turns me loose and pulls the handle up on my suitcase, grunting as she tries to lift it.

"I picked up a few things to take back."

"I hate to be the bearer of bad news," Taylor says, winking as he enters the room. Then he snags my bag from Mom and waves one arm toward the door. "But we have to go."

"On a private jet, no less," Dad says as we reach the bottom of the stairs. He extends his hand, changes his mind, and pulls Taylor in for a bear hug. "You take care of my girl."

"You have my word." Then Taylor turns and wraps his arms around my mother. "Thank you both. I'm so glad I got to meet you two."

He takes my hand as we walk down the driveway to the rental. I look at my parents and then slide inside the car.

He extends his hand, and I twine my fingers through his.

"You okay?"

"I am. I'll miss them. Knowing Dad has agreed to take better care of himself makes me worry a bit less."

"He's determined, that's for sure."

The sun will go down just about when the plane takes off. We planned the late flight to spend a few extra hours with my mom and dad. My sister will be coming home for the summer soon, so I'm comfortable she'll keep an eye on Dad.

Taylor's knuckles brush across my cheek. "I think it's convenient the plane has a bedroom. I received a text from Zack reminding me that it's small but very private."

"Did you? I'm surprised you guys talk about things like that."

"I'd bet money Morgan was the one who suggested it."

I shift in my seat at the smile on Taylor's face. "That wouldn't surprise me."

"And we *are* flying at night."

The driver pulls into a parking spot in front of the small hangar. We enter the office and work through all the security checks before boarding. The pilot is the same woman who brought me to Kauai. She chats with us about the flight and then takes our bags.

"You two make yourself comfortable."

I board and look around. The interior still smells like new leather. I sit and run my fingers over the butter-soft seats. "I could never get used to this kind of luxury."

Taylor leans around me, buckling my seat belt for me. "I hope that's not true because you deserve nothing but the best."

The captain walks down the aisle to the cockpit. Then she turns and smiles. "I have dinner on board for you when you're ready. Just help yourself. The weatherman says we'll have clear skies for the flight to Chicago. You know where the snacks and drinks are stored. Relax and enjoy the trip."

"Thank you. I think we're okay for now." Taylor looks at me, and I nod in agreement.

"We'll be in the air shortly." Then she closes the door behind her.

"Why do you think you can't get used to having money?"

I shake my head, wondering why my comment troubles him. "I live comfortably now. But just picking up the phone to say I'm going to Bora Bora, so get the plane ready? That's beyond my ability to imagine."

Then the engine revs, telling us we are getting ready to get in line for takeoff. Taylor leans back and stretches his long legs out in front of him. He turns his head toward the window and closes his eyes. I wish I knew what Taylor was thinking and how he felt.

What if Taylor doesn't want me to be in love with him?

His breathing levels out before we're even in the air. I unbuckle my seat belt and walk to the bedroom. It's small, or maybe best described as cozy. I slip off my shoes, tug my blouse from being tucked in my slacks, and stretch out.

Why did he fly to Kauai? Why should I have to get used to riches? Money has never been that important to me. Is he so ambitious that his climb toward wealth will consume him?

Too many questions run through my mind.

The compactness of the room somehow comforts me, and the soft whine of the engines almost lulls me to sleep. There is a soft knock on the door before it opens, and Taylor steps inside.

"I woke, and you weren't next to me. Funny, but I panicked even though I knew you couldn't have gone too far."

"I just needed to decompress."

He starts to back out of the room. "I'll give you some quiet time."

"Don't go." I pat the bed next to me. "I need you."

"My three favorite words." He gets on his hands and knees and crawls up the mattress to lie next to me. Then, his hand slides between my legs, rubbing the seam of my shorts against the sensitive skin. "There's not but one thing I want to taste."

"Oh God. You talk pretty."

I lift my hips in invitation. In seconds, Taylor has me naked, and he's fitting his broad shoulders between my legs. He kisses the inside of my legs and slowly works his way to the apex between my thighs.

Then his hands slip under me, lifting me toward his mouth. He kisses the top of my mound while his fingers spread me open. He curls his tongue, licking inside me as if he's starving for me. When his tongue flicks back and forth over my needy clit, the sound I make just happens, but it brings his head up.

"I don't mind if you scream. In fact, I'd like it."

I clamp a hand over my mouth and lift my hips higher. "I'll be quiet."

Chapter 15

Taylor

I close my apartment door behind me. I'm glad it's Friday. Not so much that I'm tired. I'm getting up even earlier these days because I've added a few miles to my morning run. But my brain is fried. It's also quarterly review time for many of the brokerage's clients. Most are conducted by phone, but a few of our largest clients insist on in-person meetings. Being prepped is the key to a good session, and I've spent many hours getting ready.

I haven't spent as much time as I want with Chelsea over the past few weeks. She's been stretched thin, too. She jokes that she's been training her new boss. Finally, our schedules are clear, and the weekend is ours.

I get out of my suit and tie, hang it in the closet, and call her.

"Are you still at work?" The disappointment in her voice is something I've heard often over the last two weeks, and the question guts me.

"No, ma'am. I'm on my way to the shower. Where are you?"

"Home. Why don't you throw on some jeans and a T-shirt and come over? You can spend the weekend here."

"What a smart girl you are." I pull clothes from my closet and carry them to the shower. "See you soon."

Fifteen minutes later, I head out the door. I don't tell her the real reason I came here first. I'm saving that for later at the club.

***

"Don't come up yet!" Chelsea calls right after I unlock the door and step inside her apartment.

"That wasn't exactly what I wanted to hear after not putting my hands on you for three days and long-ass nights."

"Sorry!" she calls out. I hear her feet landing on the stairs. I turn just in time to watch her naked breasts bounce with each step. I brace myself for what's coming because there's no way she can stop. I catch her just as she leaps into my arms and starts peppering kisses all over my face.

"Ooof." I fake a grunt, but her legs lock around my waist, so I bury my face in her neck and let her fresh, clean scent make this day even better. Then I slide one hand under her bare ass and run my fingers along her crack to the soft bare skin between her legs. "That's much better. Now, why couldn't I come upstairs?"

"I went shopping and was going to surprise you, but I couldn't wait." She wiggles her bottom against my fingers. "Can I just say I hate how work keeps eating away at our time together?"

"Me too. I'll make it up to you, though." I pull her mouth to mine and try to devour her. The heat from her bare skin radiates through my clothes, burning me with the need to be inside her. To own her. To hold her in my arms forever. She is intoxicating.

Her hands fumble with the zipper on my jeans. Then she moans into my mouth when she frees my cock. It's poised at her entrance, and she pulls out of our kiss.

"Please."

I lift my hips, and the head of my cock slides inside her. She's wet and warm, and I want to fill every inch of her, but I hold my position. "Is this what you want?"

"Oh, yes." Her gaze meets mine. "I needed this."

My free hand cups her breast, and her nipples pebble at my touch. I lift her and slide her down until she's impaled on my cock. My fingers skim down her spine to where we're joined, gathering moisture before reaching behind her and circling her rosebud. Her moans meet my thrusts. Her pussy is clenching down hard, and I'm going to come way too soon if I don't slow things down. Her hips push back on my hand, and my balls tighten in warning.

"Come for me, baby." I move my fingers to concentrate on her clit. I pound into her with rapid thrusts in and out. Her head drops back, and she calls my name.

"Yes. Taylor. Oh. God."

I hold her tightly while she rides out the waves. "Watching you come is beautiful."

"But—"

"Go get cleaned up. We'll see if I can keep my hands off you long enough to make the drive to the club." I slide her down my body, turn her toward the stairs, and lightly smack her ass.

"You won't peek? You'll stay down here?"

I squeeze my cock and tuck it back inside my underwear. "If you hurry."

I'm soft enough to zip my slacks when I walk to the refrigerator. I take out a bottle of water and chug it. Then I return to the living room and pace. She's doing something special for me, and I can't wait to see it.

"I'm ready."

I turn, and every drop of blood in my body runs south. My fingers open and close as if they have a mind of their own. "Fuck me. You're stunning."

"Really? It's not too much?" She tugs at the bottom, but there's no use. "Well, it's not too little?"

I quickly cross the room. "Turn around."

She sucks her bottom lip in between her teeth and slowly does a three-sixty. She has pulled her hair into a high ponytail, baring her shoulders. The black latex dress appears to be painted on her body. Spaghetti straps hold up a top that barely covers her delicious nipples, and a zipper runs from between her breasts to the bottom, which will make removing it a snap. My mouth dries up, and I clear my throat and swallow.

"Say something."

"You are the most beautiful creature on earth." I hold out my hands and watch as hers cover my palms. "You've changed me by simply being you. You're the most loving, adventurous, exciting, and positive person I've ever met. That you're willing to try anything with me and for me makes me love you even more."

Her eyes widened, tears formed in them, and they ran down her cheeks like water over a broken dam. Then she pulls her hands from mine and wipes her face. Black swipes of mascara streak across her cheeks.

"You just said you love me."

"I seem to remember saying that." I thumb at the black streaks on her face, making it worse. But she's beautiful anyway. Did I speak too soon and fuck this up? "Is that a problem?"

"No. It's a really good thing."

"Because? Am I going to have to drag the words out of you?"

"No, Sir. I love you, too. With every fiber of my being, I love you."

"Thank fuck." I kiss her, slamming my mouth against her so hard our teeth clack. Our tongues finish expressing our thoughts, and at least for a few minutes, sex doesn't cross my mind. A warm peace settles inside my heart, and I know who has claimed that space as hers.

She finally leans back and looks up at me. "Give me a minute to fix my face, and then we can go to the club. Okay?"

I kiss her gently this time. "We're not going anywhere but up those stairs, where I'm going to peel that dress off you and show you all the different ways to say I love you."

Chapter 16

Chelsea

His soft lips kiss the tip of my nose, my lips, and between my breasts. Needing to touch him, I test my restraints.

Taylor chuckles. "Going somewhere?"

"No, Sir. Not even if I could."

"Patience has its rewards, you know."

He checks the blindfold covering my eyes, the soft leather cuffs securing my wrists to the table, and then the bindings holding my legs bent at the knees. I'm spread wide open. I'm his to do with however he desires. That alone has my juices flowing in anticipation. His hands are making trails all over my body. He's touching me while he kisses and nips my bare skin.

"Oh my God," I moan and try to lift my hips as an offering.

His lips suck my nipple into his mouth while his fingers pull and pinch the other one. Then he works his way down my body, stopping at my mound and tonguing the tip of my clit. I feel the straps around my thighs tighten, spreading me even wider.

"Beautiful," he whispers before running his hands down the inside of my thighs.

He flicks my clit back and forth. My skin is more sensitive to his touch today. I'm considering begging as a tactic until a finger slides deep inside me and pumps in and out.

My breath catches. *What's happening?* My clit and my breasts are both being tortured by a tongue.

I freeze. "Taylor?"

"I'm right here, love." He kisses me. "Relax, and let us pleasure you."

"Us?"

"Shh."

Whoever it is, the two of them are relentless. They knead, suck, and lash me while somebody's finger is fucking me. I thrash against the restraints.

"Ohhhh. I can't stop it."

"Come now."

I virtually explode. Taylor whispers words of love while I ride out the orgasm as wave after wave of bliss slams into me. He releases my wrist restraints and then my legs as he pulls me into his arms.

Then he slides the blindfold off my head, and I look around the room. It's just the two of us. Covering my eyes had been a good idea, because I don't know if I could've relaxed enough to come with two men watching. I started to ask the name of the other man, but I wasn't sure I wanted to know.

"I promised we'd check off everything you said you'd be interested in trying."

I snuggle close to him. "Yes, you did."

"I need to feel your skin as I slide inside of you. To be touching you when I come."

"I want that, too." I cup his face in my hands. "I swear you can almost talk me into an orgasm." His tongue traces my lips, licks the corners, and then plunges inside my mouth. I love his taste and touch. He's a fantastic kisser, and I will never have enough of him.

Then his hand slides between my legs, and discovers how wet I am. He sinks a finger inside me, removes it, and then paints my lips.

I slide my tongue across, tasting myself. I share by kissing him. "That's what you do to me."

His eyes never leave mine as he releases me and helps me get in position. "I love you."

He quickly strips. I watch as his erection pops free of his underwear. He's just too handsome for words, so I turn on the table and wrap my hand around him. "Let me taste you."

"How can I refuse?"

I open my mouth and slide him deep inside. I moan and pull him deeper as I move back and forth. I put all my weight on one hand and cup his balls.

"Fuck." He pulls out and steps back. He opens a drawer and takes a bottle of lube out. The lid pops open. He pours some into his hand and then strokes himself.

"That is so sexy."

"Turn around. Head and shoulders down."

I get into position but tense when drops of cold liquid hit my bare skin. He runs one finger around and around my hole, taking his time, relaxing me until sliding inside of me is easy. Sensations, hot and tingly, circulate through my body. I want what he wants; thank God he wants me, too. He places one hand on my lower back. The other guides his dick to my rear entrance. We've been here before, but he always ensures I'm ready.

"Remember. Push against me like you're trying to keep me out."

The head edges its way just inside me. The worst part is over, but Taylor stops to let me adjust.

"My God, you are tight. Try not to tense up. Relax."

I nod. "Relax" is my mantra for a few seconds as Taylor pushes forward, going deeper into my ass.

"Color."

"Green, Sir."

He holds me still as he slowly moves in and out of me. "You're doing great. Are you ready for more?"

"Yes, please." My interior muscles rebel at the intrusion, and it stings, but not for long, and not enough for me to stop him. I know how good this is going to be.

He moves deeper until I feel his hips flush against me. "You feel so good. Squeeze me."

I tighten my sphincter muscles and revel in his loud moan. I look over my shoulder and watch his face as his hips move in a slow and easy motion. I can't understand the need that washes over me, but it's not enough. I need more. "Sir?"

"Yes?"

"Are you all the way in? I never feel this full until right before I ask you to fuck me hard."

His hips flex, and he smiles down at me. "So much for nice and easy?"

"More, please. Harder." Then he slams into me, soon finding the perfect rhythm. He strokes past that delicious spot that has me moving faster, and I'm lost in bliss.

"Fuck," he growls. "I never want to stop fucking you."

"Yellow," I cry out. "I can't stop it." My spine starts to tingle as my orgasm starts moving through me. "I'm too close."

He rests his weight on one arm and slides his hand under me to my clit. Gathering moisture, he slathers it on me before pinching and rubbing hard and fast.

"Come. I want to feel you come before I fill your ass."

I'm pretty sure I scream. I don't think I've ever done it before during sex, but I'm sure it will happen again. My vision blurs as he continues to pump into me, causing a second orgasm to rush in behind the first.

"Fuck!" he roars like an enraged beast. "I fucking love you."

I feel him come, warm liquid bathing my insides. The world stalls until he slowly turns us onto our sides, facing each other. We're soaking wet with sweat, breathing like there's no tomorrow, and grinning like fools.

He kisses me. "I never expected to love anyone as much as I do you."

"I'm so glad you do. I've been in love with you for a while."

He stands and grabs a tub of wet wipes.

I roll onto my back and watch as he cleans me as tenderly as if I'm fine china. After he cleaned himself, he helped me put on my dress. I wish I'd bought a new one for tonight, but I've built quite a clubwear wardrobe over the past few months. Taylor dresses quickly and then kneels and slides my shoes on for me.

He takes my hand, and we start out of the room. I stop and look at him.

He has to know this question is coming.

"Who was in the room with us earlier?"

Taylor pulls me against his chest. "There are only three men in the world I would trust to touch your body, and that's only if I'm in the room."

It takes mere seconds for me to process what he is telling me. No way would he ask Zack or Nick because of Morgan and Kayla. "Slider?"

"He's a little concerned that if the others find out, it might cause friction."

"No one has to know." I stand up on my tiptoes and kiss Taylor. "It was something we three experienced together."

When we get to the club, he takes my hand as we walk up front. We stop at a booth. "I'll leave you here just long enough to order drinks and text Gabriel."

I slide into the booth to wait. "Water for me, please."

"I should've thought of that."

Slider comes out of the office just as Taylor starts toward the bar. Their conversation only lasts a moment. I can see he's uncomfortable as he returns and hands me a water bottle.

"He wants to speak with you for a minute."

"Not if you're against it. I love you. Period."

"He wants to make sure things aren't uncomfortable every time we're together. I won't tell you what you should do, but I'll support whatever you decide."

"You won't be gone long?"

"No, I won't."

"Okay. Let's clear the air."

He walks away, and my heart swells. That he trusts me to have this conversation means a lot. I straighten my spine and try not to appear embarrassed as Slider heads my way.

He sits across from me with his back to the bar. "This may be a little awkward, but it has to happen."

"I appreciate you for helping Taylor satisfy my curiosity."

"I wondered if he'd tell you."

"I asked him who the other man was. He trusts you." Having this conversation is more difficult than I expected. Not long ago, this man's head was buried between my legs. "You're a good guy who helped out a friend."

Slider coughs a couple of times. His blue eyes darken as he leans back into the booth. "Darlin', I am not, never have been, and will never be 'a good guy.' I wanted you. I wouldn't pass up the chance to taste what I'll never have. But I'm also a proud bastard, and I accept that you belong to Taylor."

"I do. I love him very much. No one needs to know what the three of us shared. I don't want any tension when we're all together."

"Good enough." Slider slides out of the booth. "Thanks."

Taylor is motioning to me as he crosses the floor. I stand and walk to meet him. My heart filled with happiness, and my steps got faster as I neared him. He wraps his arms around me. "Are you okay?"

"As long as you love me, I'll be just fine."

"Then we have no problems."

"None."

"Our ride is ready."

"So am I. Let's go home."

Epilogue

Three months later

I stand in the doorway and watch the moving van drive away, leaving Chelsea and me surrounded by dozens of boxes. She wraps her arms around me and rests her head between my shoulder blades.

"How come they did all the work, and *I'm* exhausted?"

I kiss the top of her head. "Nerves. Moving in together is stressful."

"Moving, yes. Living with you is not."

I take her hand, and we turn to survey the beginnings of our new life. "At least they packed our stuff. Now we have to figure out where everything is and where it goes."

"Let's start with the bedroom first," she says.

"Another reason I love you."

"Because I chose the bedroom to unpack first?"

"Think about it. The moving guys assembled the bed and put the mattress on it before they left. Let's officially christen our new place." I toss her over my shoulder. With her squealing and laughing, I carry her to our new bedroom and put her feet on the floor. "Strip."

She's still laughing while she sheds her clothes. Then she jumps on the bed. "Hurry. You have some work to do."

I undress and crawl halfway up her body. "Hmm. My work begins here." My hands lift her hips so high her back is off the bed, and her weight is on her shoulders. "Perfect."

"You love me?" she asks.

"More than the air I breathe. More than life itself." I kiss the top of her mound. "Was that enough syrupy talk?"

I don't wait for her answer. Instead, I sink my face into her and set about pleasuring the woman I'm going to call my wife. My tongue draws a line from her asshole to her clit before lapping at her entrance. Over and over, I suck at her tender flesh. Chelsea digs her heels into the bed and rocks against my mouth while I devour her. I want inside her.

My cock. My fingers. My tongue. Chelsea is a fucking drug, and I can't get enough of her.

"Don't stop," she begs.

"No fucking way. I'm addicted to you." I lower her hips to the bed and roll her on top of me in one move. "It's your turn. Make me come."

Her eyes widen. I've never given her control, but today is special.

"With pleasure." Her hand wraps around my cock and lines me up before she slowly, achingly, lowers herself.

My hands cover her breasts, kneading the warm flesh. Her nipples pebble, and I pull her closer so I can nip and suckle. Her movements are fast as she presses against my pubic bone. She sits up, leans back, and places her hands on my thighs. My cock is as far inside her body as it can go. I slide one hand between us and capture her clit.

Her gaze locks on mine as she rides me hard. Her hips slide up, back, and in circles until we both cry out together. When she collapses on my chest, I don't turn us onto our sides. Instead, we just are. We exist in a place we share with no one else.

I could stay here, inside her, forever.

Her breathing eventually slows, and I stay very still until I'm sure she's asleep. Then I ease her off me. She mewls like a cat and curls up without waking.

I could watch her sleep for hours, but work was waiting for me. I quickly dress and go downstairs. I move all the boxes to one side and then arrange the living room furniture. A quick trip to my car, and I retrieve my surprises from the trunk. Soon, I had champagne on ice, two silver flutes with my last name embossed on them, and candles strategically placed on the coffee table.

So far, so good.

I go back upstairs and strip before digging out bathroom necessities. Then I join her on the bed. "Nap time is over, Sleeping Beauty."

She rolls onto her back and stretches. Her naked body pulls at me, and I'm getting hard as stone.

"Doesn't she get woken by her true love's kiss?"

"Don't encourage me, or we'll never get unpacked." I lean down and cover her lips with mine. I keep it soft and gentle, giving her just enough to motivate her. "Let's try out the new shower."

"Hmm. Not an entirely bad idea." She laughs up at me. "We need towels, though."

"I've got you covered." I get up and walk into the bathroom. The shower here is twice as large as her old apartment and at least four times the size of mine. I turn all the jets on and set the water to warm. I don't wait for her. The desire to see her face light up outweighs my carnal need for now. I'm getting out just as she steps in.

"You didn't wait for me."

Fuck, she's making it hard not to christen the shower. "We've got food in ice coolers. I'll get started putting it in the fridge." I dig through a box marked "hanging clothes" and pull out some sweats and a t-shirt before heading downstairs.

I pace across the living room floor to the couch and stand beside it. Then, I wait. And wait. She's taking her time, and I'm having a nervous breakdown.

"Are you coming downstairs anytime soon?"

"Why are you hurrying me?"

I'm standing at the bottom of the stairs when she bounces down them. She glances around and then up at me.

"You've been busy."

"I thought we'd have a glass of champagne." I take her hand and escort her to the living room. "Have a seat."

"Champagne and candles? You'll spoil me."

I pop the top on the bubbly, fill both flutes and hand her one. "I fully intend to."

She holds the flute up to the light. "They're beautiful."

I can't wait any longer. I lower myself to one knee, pull out the small ring box I had tucked inside my pocket, and look into her beautiful eyes.

"I love you with all that I am or ever will be. If you do me the honor of being my wife, I'll never stop trying to make you happy. Will you marry me?"

She cups my cheeks in her small hands, leans down, and whispers, "Yes. Yes. Yes. Yes."

I slip the diamond ring on her finger, stand, and pull her off the couch into my arms. Her legs lock around me. Tears are leaving little trails down her cheeks.

"Happy tears?"

"*Very* happy tears."

I lean over, blow out the candles, and pick up the bottle of champagne. "Grab those two flutes."

She stretches and snags them both. "I noticed they both had your last name on them. Chelsea Horne does have a nice ring to it."

Read on for a sneak peek of book four.

COME UNDONE

Come Undone

Prologue

Kenzie

"No. No. No. Not now." I'm yelling at a dying car, and it's not helping. After a rapid series of sputters, shudders, and coughs, my eleven-year-old vehicle, which has been on its last legs for a while, dies.

Steering to the shoulder of the road is good in theory, but I have no power steering without the engine running. My arm muscles scream as I put everything I have into coasting this baby onto the shoulder of the road. When I finally stop rolling, I put on the emergency brake, turn on my emergency flashers, unhook my seat belt, and hop out.

I about jump out of my skin as a car zips past, and the driver honks at me. Okay, I thought about flipping him off but didn't. Technically the ass end of my car is off the road. You can call it barely, but in this case, it barely counts. It's not like I'm blocking a lane. I pop the hood and raise it. I don't know what I'm looking at or for, but I stare for a minute.

I think through my options, which are few. There's not much help available on the busy highway. Cars are speeding by as if in a hurry to be somewhere. Sweat breaks and runs between my boobs, soaking the band of my bra. I pull out my phone and stare at it as if a name and number will magically appear. It's five o'clock on a Friday, and everyone I know either doesn't own a car or is headed home from work.

Work. Crap. My stomach clenches. Tonight's a big night at the steak house where I work. Not only will I miss earning some badly needed tips, but this is one of the busiest nights of the weekend for the restaurant.

My friend from school, Meg Tilton, is the most likely to be at home by now. Before I can pull up her name, the deep rumble of a motorcycle drowns out my thoughts.

The man stops, kills the engine, and uses the big black boot he's wearing to drop the kickstand. He slings a leg over the tank, gets off, and removes his helmet.

I usually think bikers are hot as hell, but not today. His long hair is stringy, the wife-beater he's wearing was probably white at one time, and his jeans could use a thorough washing.

"Looks like I found myself a damsel in distress." His eyes slide over me, stopping at my breasts. "Those long legs will wrap around my..."

I arch my eyebrows at him.

"Bike just fine."

He doesn't understand personal space because he keeps coming toward me. I step back only to find myself wedged between him and my car. The smell of alcohol and unwashed body parts reaches me before he does. "I appreciate you stopping, but a friend is coming to pick me up. Thanks anyway."

He ignores my subtle dismissal and steps closer. "Bullshit. I'll take you anywhere you want to go. We'll stop for a drink on the way."

"No, really. My boyfriend will be here in a few minutes."

Biker Guy sways, looking unsteady on his feet. I'm thinking I can outrun him, but where would I go? Cars fly down the highway, and nobody is paying attention to me.

His eyes narrow. "He's ain't much of a boyfriend letting you drive that broken-down piece of shit."

"It has sentimental value." He's bad-mouthing my car, and it's pissing me off. I can't vouch for the first five years, but she's been a good ride for the past six. I tap the nine on my phone but pause when a shiny silver Corvette pulls over and stops. All I can tell is that the driver is male, and that's all I need to know right now. "There he is."

I scoot around Biker Guy and run to the good Samaritan, who is getting out of his car. I don't give him a chance to close the door before I wrap my arms around him and pull him in for a hug.

"Honey." I look up into his face and talk loud enough to get over the low din of the highway. "I'm glad you finally got here."

Amusement flits across the guy's face, and his mouth curves into a half-smile. All my words vanish. Heat shoots up my face, and I release him as if he were on fire. My fingers itch, and I clasp them together to keep them from unbuttoning his shirt and checking for a giant red S on his undershirt. Okay, I know he's not that guy but holy shit.

Tall with broad shoulders, black hair, and eyes the color of the Caribbean Sea, he takes my breath away. The tailored black suit he's wearing fits like a glove. I feel his muscles ripple as he steps back, tilts his head, and looks down at me. At this point, he knows I'm staring.

His gaze sweeps the scene before him, no doubt trying to understand the situation he's gotten himself into. His muscular arm slides around my waist and pulls me closer. "I got here as fast as I could. Let's take a look at your car."

I nod my response as another run of sweat slides down my chest. After standing out in the sun, I issue a silent prayer that I don't smell like Biker Guy. His arm guides me over to my car, and he smiles.

"Thanks for stopping to help my woman. Looks like no one else was willing to take the time. I appreciate it."

"You ain't much of a boyfriend if you drive a fucking Vette and let your woman drive a piece of shit."

Unfazed, Vette Guy nods. "You're probably right, but what she drives isn't your concern, is it?" He lowers the hood on my car. "I'll have this one towed."

Male testosterone is getting thicker by the second while these two bulls stare each other down. I lift and kiss Vette Guy on the cheek. The disruptive tactic works because both men look at me.

"Honey, we need to get going."

"Me too. I've got business to take care of." Biker Guy climbs aboard his bike, and the engine roars to life within seconds. He revs the engine, and dust flies from under his tires. I swear the ground shakes under my feet.

"Thank you." I cough, waving my hand in front of my face. Reluctantly, I remove myself from Vette Guy's arm and take my cell out to call Meg. "You can go too. I'll be fine."

"Really?" He flashes straight white teeth at me. "After all we've been through?"

"I'm afraid so."

"Are you calling family?"

My spine automatically stiffens. "No," I snap. "I truly appreciate you stopping. It could have gotten ugly. But I'm fine now. Okay?"

"No. It's not okay. I'm not leaving you out here for easy picking. Remember the asshole who just left? There's more where he came from." The timbre of his voice tells me he's made up his mind. "I'm happy to take you wherever you were headed."

"I don't know you. Granted, you smell better than he did, but you could be a serial killer for all I know. Thank you for stopping, but I can take care of myself."

"Justin Locke. Pleased to meet you." He blows out a huff of air as if I've offended him. Before I can react, my cell is in his hand. He snaps a picture of his license plate, takes a selfie, and texts himself. "You can send those three pictures to that friend you were going to call and tell her if you're not in touch within the hour, call the cops."

Both sides of my brain kick in, and the battle of whether I stay or go is off and running.

"Not enough?" He pulls his wallet from his hip pocket, removes his driver's license, takes a shot of it, and hands my cell back to me.

"Now, will you get in the car?"

"Bossy much?"

One corner of his mouth lifts into a grin. "You have no idea."

He makes me weak in the knees. I have a hard time believing he'd have to boss anybody around. With his looks, I have no doubt he can ask for and get what he wants.

"You're as safe with me as I am with you." He walks to his car, opens the door, and waits. "I'm not leaving you here by yourself. Get in."

I grab my purse from my car's passenger seat and my uniform hanging in the back. The furrow between his brows and the thin line his lips formed relaxed when I slammed the door closed on my car, patted the roof, said goodbye, and joined him.

"Did you just talk to an inanimate object?"

"I did. You have a problem with that?"

"Not even one." He's looking at me as if I've escaped a madhouse.

"That car and I have been through a lot together." I have no idea why I'm defending my behavior. Yes, I do. He's too pushy.

"In."

He catches my elbow, and I allow him to steady me as I lower all five foot-eight inches of my body into his car. It's one of those automobiles that sit inches above the ground, causing my entrance to be less than graceful. How any woman wearing a dress can get in or out of this car without flashing the world is a mystery. One I won't have to solve.

He closes the door, walks around, and slides in behind the steering wheel. A second later, the Vette rumbles to life. The sound reminds me of a big cat purring—a very big, very angry cat.

"Where to?"

I extend my right hand. "Since we both could be in danger, we should probably know each other's names. I'm Kenzie Stone."

"As I said before, Justin Locke." He rewards me with another of his half-smiles as his hand swallows mine. His grip is firm, and I like that he didn't grasp my fingertips and wiggle them. "Where to?" he asks again.

I give him the address of my apartment complex and watch as he taps into the information with his long, thick fingers. He's a big guy and tall enough that I have to tilt my head back to look up at him. That doesn't happen often. He drives into traffic and quickly navigates to the fast lane.

"I appreciate your help."

"You're welcome. My grandfather would spin in his grave if I ignored a woman stranded anywhere. Much less a beautiful woman."

I ignore that last part because I keep my hair tied back and makeup to a minimum while at work. "Your grandfather must have been a good man."

"He was."

We ride in the uncomfortable silence of two total strangers for a few minutes. I decide to ask questions. "What do you do for a living?"

"I'm the Director of Technology for a major retail company."

"So you're off work for the weekend, and I shouldn't feel too guilty about keeping you from being somewhere, right?"

"Close but not one hundred percent accurate. I'm also co-owner of an adult-only club, and tonight's the grand opening."

"Somehow, I don't think you're referring to a Country Club, are you?"

"No. It's a place where people who live a certain lifestyle can be comfortable, and no one passes judgment."

"A sex club?"

"Exactly." Justin glances at me. "Did I detect a note of curiosity in your question?"

"You did not." He's gorgeous, has money, and is way out of my league. That doesn't stop me from wondering how his hands would feel on my body after he'd handcuffed me.

"Sounded like it to me. How much do you know about BDSM?"

My jaw comes unhinged. Is he reading my mind? "I read."

"In other words, nothing." He changes lanes, accelerates, and speeds past a slower-moving car.

"It's not my major, so I admit you're right. My knowledge of the subject is limited."

"You shouldn't rely on romance novels for information. If you're the least curious, it's best to see firsthand."

My brain shifts into overload, and the blood in my veins heats up at the thought of what he means by 'firsthand.' I've read lots of romance books with BDSM, mafia bosses, and men in general who dominate women. The stories serve as a constant reminder I don't have time for a sex life. I can't discuss his lifestyle. Not when he makes me wonder what having an orgasm is like. Well, one that's not self-induced.

"If that's an invitation, no thanks. Between work and college, sex isn't my top priority."

"What are you studying?"

I breathe easier when the subject changes suddenly. "I'm going to be a paralegal when I grow up. If I stay the course, I'll take the exam with The Association for Legal Professionals around my twenty-fifth birthday."

"Good for you." He reaches over and pats my shoulder. "If my first impression of you is right, you'll succeed."

"Thanks."

"You snapped at me when I mentioned family. You're not close?"

"I might be if I had any."

"That had to be tough." He glances at me when I don't respond. "You're street exit is next. You have someone to help with your car?"

"I do." I'm relieved when he doesn't pry.

"Good." He guides the car to the outside lane and shoots down the ramp and off the freeway. A couple of blocks later, he drove through the gate and stopped in front of my building.

"Thank you so much. I'll pay it forward." I unbuckle, hop out, and grab my stuff, happy not to answer any more questions.

"It was my pleasure. See you around."

I close the car door and hurry inside. I don't understand his effect on me, but my heart hasn't stopped racing since I gave him the fake kiss. I hate to see him drive away. I stop, turn inside the stairwell, and watch until his sports car is out of sight. I jog up the stairs, smiling. How many women can say a superhero saved them?

I call work, and if I can work a double shift tomorrow, all will be forgiven. I jump on that because it will help pay for using the bus system since the train doesn't run this route. My stomach rolls into a knot. I hadn't considered how much my car was going to cost. I'll have to dip into what little savings I have. If that doesn't cover the price, the balance has to go to my credit card.

I walk into the kitchen, grab a coffee cup, and fill it with red wine. Carrying it to the living room, I sit on the couch, take out my cell, and try to locate a company to haul my car to a garage. The first few places I call are closed but have an emergency phone number. Can I afford the extra charge? I refuse to stress any more than I am already doing, but I keep looking. Those who aren't closed need a destination to deliver the car to, and I don't know of a garage nearby.

I stop searching. Tomorrow, somebody at work will know who I need to contact. I fix a sandwich, slip on a pair of sleep shorts and a T-shirt, and spread my homework across my bed.

****

My alarm jars me awake, and I discover my laptop is still on, and my head rests on an open book. I haven't accomplished as much as I'd planned. Rolling out of bed, I save what little work I'd completed before falling asleep and go to the kitchen. The restaurant doesn't serve breakfast, so I have a few hours to kill. I fix myself a cup of coffee and start my weekend washing clothes and getting ready for the upcoming week.

It's after lunch before I shower and dress in shorts and a tank top. I finally have time to work on my unfinished homework, so I grab my laptop, open my patio door, and sit at the small round table in the corner. My view is of the parking lot, but I'm happy with that for now.

It's warm again today, and the sun feels good on my skin. The urge to slip on my bathing suit and hit the pool is strong, but the need to finish this assignment is stronger. I stand to refill my cup and notice a beige Ford pulling into the parking lot. It's exactly like mine. I walk to the iron railing and watch my car pull into an empty slot right in front of the entrance to the building.

What the hell? I'm barefoot, but that doesn't stop me racing through my living room, down the stairs, and outside. I arrive just in time to watch a second car drive away. I'm guessing with the driver. The hot pavement stings my feet, but I can't turn back. I run open the door and get inside.

It takes a second before I realize I'd left my car on the side of the road with the key in the ignition. He'd had her towed and repaired? I start my poor old friend, and she hums to life. I turn off the engine and sit here.

Justin's kindness overwhelms me. I don't know how to react. How to feel. I take care of myself and have done so since I was six. People don't do things for me unless there's something in it for them. Tears fill my eyes and spill down my cheeks. I can't remember the last time I cried.

I spot a white envelope on the passenger seat. I pick it up and carefully open it. Inside is an embossed invitation to Club Satin to be used on my twenty-fifth birthday. The only instruction is to ask for Slider.

About the Author

A student of creative writing in her youth, Jerrie set aside her passion when life presented her with a John Wayne husband and a wonderful daughter. Her love for romantic suspense inspires her to write alpha males and kick-ass women. Her characters weave their way through death and danger to emerge stronger, because of, and on occasion, in spite of, their love for each other. If they're tough enough, they live happily ever after.

Jerrie lives in Texas, denies having an accent, thrives on sunshine, children's laughter, sugar (human and granulated), and researching for her heroes and heroines. She loves to hear from her readers. Find a complete list of her books at http://www.jerriealexander.com or contact her at jerrie@jerriealexander.com.

Read more at www.jerriealexander.com.

9 798227 682024